CREATION WAITS FOR WHO?

CREATION WAITS FOR WHO?

Anne Elmer

Editions de la Source
Neauphle le Château
France

Published and Administrated in France by Editions de la Source, in partnership with The Elijah List, Albany, OR, USA.

Editions de la Source	The Elijah List
2 Chemin des Ecarts	528 Ellsworth St. SW
Neauphle le Château	Albany, OR 97321
France	USA

Cover by : Christian Design and Print, Nottingham, England
Printed in the USA by : Versa Press, Inc.
1465 Spring Bay Rd.
East Peoria, IL 61611-9788

ISBN 978-2-917973-28-8
Dépôt légal (Paris) 2 Q 2013

"Creation is waiting for He who is within YOU to be revealed to the world, and the Spirit is ready to lead you into the fullness of your calling. Anne powerfully encourages us to choose this life, helping us understand the immense power and possibility God is waiting for us to step into. She is empowering us all to live out the powerful nature of a real "son", thus revealing God's nature to the world. Anne does a wonderful job at placing the choice before us, teaching us through the promises, and leading us into that choice, and life, that will transform the world around us - simply by choosing to be who the Father has already created us to be."

Joey LeTourneau

Author of ***Revolutionary Freedom* & *The Life Giver***

Acknowledgments

There are many I could name who have helped me through to this point in getting this book in print, but the list would be long. However, three of my very best friends have excelled themselves in support and encouragement, I name them here.

Thanks must go first and foremost to Jesus, my Lord and my very best friend. I couldn't and I wouldn't have done it without His initiative, and His constant companionship. Thankyou Lord for everything you are.

After Him, there are two others, both wonderful friends and prayer partners, who must be highlighted. Gerry Raymond took her professional scalpel to my humble efforts and made something beautiful and presentable. Thanks Gerry for your enthusiasm and for your love and support.

The other is my husband Malgwyn, who is also the publisher of the French book. He has sat through hundred's of my sermons and is expert at keeping me on track. Thankyou for who you are, and for always being there.

Before We Start

One thing I would like to highlight before we start is that I have written about "sons of God" and "Sons of God" or in later chapters "Real Sons of God". The capitalization refers to those end-time Sons of God that creation is waiting for. In order to illustrate my point I have taken the liberty of changing to capital letters some of the Bible references to "sons of God".

I have put all Bible references in full, so that those who are not accustomed to reading the Bible will not have to deal with unfamiliar abbreviations. I have also inserted most Bible verses in full, and in the case of the Luke 15 passage, the whole story because of one of my own failings. I am one who often sees a Bible reference in a book, and either I presume I know what it says, or I think I will read it later, and then I forget or I don't get round to it. Reading the references in full is very important to the message of this book, because in most cases, we are not talking generalities, and we need to know what the Lord is actually saying, not what we suppose He might be saying.

My prayer is that the reader makes the prayerful decision to become one of the Sons of God that creation is waiting for, and that creation won't have to wait too much longer. Be blessed and encouraged as you read.

Contents

Chapter 1

Invitation To An Adventure

The title of this book just dropped into my spirit one afternoon as I was sitting in Kansas City airport on my way home at the end of a six week ministry tour of the US. I did not know until that moment that I was even going to write a book on this subject! The Lord broke into my musings which were about nothing in particular, other than going home, and said "The title of your next book is 'Creation waits for who?'" I have never considered myself a writer; my first book "Transported by the Lion of Judah"[1] happened much more by accident than by design, but then I know that the Lord designs our accidents, so I trust Him with everything.

I didn't realize it, but what the Lord was doing was inviting me to go on an adventure with Him. It was to be a steep learning process, and a lot of fun. Writing the book has been an adventure, and being in the process of becoming one of the Sons of God for the last-days is an on-going adventure. But sitting in the airport that day, I knew none of that, and was more concerned with the

[1] *Transported by The Lion of Judah*
published in the USA by The Elijah List and in Europe by Editions de la Source, France

grammatical construction of what the Lord had just told me.

My response to His command to write was: "You cannot use that title, "Creation waits for who?" is not correct. It should be "whom" not "who" at least in British English, but He did not instruct or allow me to change the grammar, so I supposed it was not one of His priorities, and consequently must not be one of mine. My apologies to any linguistic purists among my readers, please forgive me and if this broken rule bothers you, then may I ask you to take up the issue with the God who created the language we speak and read, and who also gave me the title.

The tour I had just finished began just outside Chicago, in a small town which has a youth church meeting on Friday evenings. That church was my first speaking engagement of a tour that was to take me to six US states in as many weeks. During the night before the meeting, the Lord woke me and told me to speak on the difference between the two types of sons of God mentioned in Romans 8 verses 14 and 19, verses I had never even contemplated before that night.

> Romans 8:14 *...because those who are led by the Spirit of God are sons of God.*

> Romans 8:19 *The creation waits in eager expectation for the Sons of God to be revealed.*

What is the difference between these two sorts of sons of God? And what exactly is creation waiting for? These are the questions I tried to answer in that hastily prepared message, and they are the questions which I am still trying to answer in this book.

Another task the Lord gave me in that Illinois church, was to anoint all those under the age of 30 as the "last generation." I spoke very briefly on this subject that evening in Chicago, before obeying the Lord and anointing with oil each one of those who were in the appropriate age group.

Later during that US tour, again in direct obedience to the Lord, I was led to give the same anointing to one other group of young people: a group of young dancers in a church in Missouri. Since that time, I have had the same message and anointing for a few other individuals. The first was a young Englishman whom I met while staying with friends in central France. The second was a young French pianist who was playing with a worship group in a prayer conference for Europe which took place in Brussels. The Lord also arranged a meeting with a young couple who are evangelists working with street kids in Ethiopia. They too were anointed by the Lord as Last-Days Sons; it was a powerful moment. Several months later, the Lord instructed me to anoint and pray for a group of under-thirties at a new church plant in Johannesburg while on a South African tour.

Each time I have anointed someone in this way, there has been a powerful presence of the Holy Spirit, and the anointing was administered in direct obedience to the Lord. It has never been done lightly, and it has never been received lightly. To be called out as one of the Sons of God for the last generation demands a great deal of commitment, and is not to be taken lightly in any way.

After receiving the invitation from God to look deeper into this subject, I have gone on to study more of what the Bible tells us of the expectations of the Lord for this "end-time generation". This book is the result of that search.

I believe I have barely scratched the surface, but I hope to give my readers a taste of what a Real Son of God (RSG) is, and I pray that each of you is encouraged to dig deeper for yourself into this whole matter. Even if you are over the age of 30, you can still be an RSG, and as you will see in one of the later chapters, the parents, godparents and mentors of this generation have a great responsibility too.

Chapter 2

Led By The Spirit Of God

Romans 8:14 *...those who are led by the Spirit of God are sons of God.*

Most of the Christians I know, myself included, can identify with this statement. I know that I am a son of God, and I know that I am led by the spirit of God, at least a lot of the time. I know in my heart, as well as in the "theological" part of my brain, that the Holy Spirit is trying to lead me all the time. However, I have to admit to not yet being able to listen 24/7, even if that is my desire and my goal.

I have learned, in my Christian walk, that while the Lord often speaks through an individual verse, it is not usually wise to take any verse out of its context, so we will look at the verse quoted above with its preceding verses. I have also learned that the word of God is living and active *(Hebrews 4:12),* which means that it can mean something for the reader one day, and bring light in a completely different direction the next day. As I meditate on scripture, I ask the Lord to give me layer upon layer of revelation and understanding. I hope the reader will not just accept my interpretation of Bible verses as absolute truth, but will search deeper into the meaning of everything taken from The Word of God, allowing the Holy Spirit to bring greater personal revelation.

Keeping this in mind let us look at the context of our verse quoted above.

> Romans 8: 12-14 *Therefore, brothers, we have an obligation-but it is not to the sinful nature, to live according to it. For if you live according to the sinful nature, you will die; but if by the Spirit you put to death the misdeeds of the body, you will live, because those who are led by the Spirit of God are sons of God.*

Reading these verses makes me think of a basic conversion experience, when as people become believers and decide to follow Christ, or in other words, follow the Spirit of God. They repent of past sins and make a conscious decision to die to self and live for Christ. From that moment on, they hope and expect to be led by the Holy Spirit. So I imagine that all those believers who have made a commitment to the Lord, or have had a conversion experience at some time in their lives can identify with this verse, and say "Yes, I am led by the Spirit of God," at least for part of the time, if not all day, every day.

Let's go back to our Bible verse again, and work through it a bit more slowly.

> Romans 8:12-14 *Therefore, brothers,...*

I remember a long time ago, when I was first getting into Bible study, and I was devouring every piece of advice that I could about understanding the Word of God, we had a visiting preacher in our church. At one point in the sermon the speaker read a Bible verse which began with "therefore". She promptly stopped, looked around at the listening group and said: "If ever you see a 'therefore' in the Bible, you should look what it is there for!" I have never forgotten that advice, and have been encouraged to read more and to dig deeper into many Bible passages. Because the passage quoted above starts with "therefore", we need to go back a bit further in the chapter, and see what the "therefore" is there for.

> Romans 8:10-11 *But if Christ is in you, your body is dead because of sin, yet your spirit is alive because of righteousness. And if the Spirit of Him who raised Jesus from the dead is living in you, He who raised Christ from the dead will also give life to your mortal bodies through His Spirit, who lives in you.*

So often in Paul's letters he seems to be speaking in riddles, and yet if we cut them up into "bite-sized" pieces, and meditate on them long enough, the Lord always brings clarity. Here we see that although the body is dead, the spirit is alive, and because the spirit is alive then the body is too.

Here is how I interpret these verses:

As I became a Christian, I recognised that my body deserved to die because of the sinful nature, or the soulish nature that had ruled my life until that point. But once I took Jesus into my heart, my spirit became alive and started to rule instead of my soul, which had been very much in charge of my daily life before that meeting with the Lord. The result of my spirit being alive means that my body is more alive than it ever was before. I now use my mortal body to live for Jesus as long as He allows me to stay on the earth.

Thus I have the possibility to live my life totally for Him. I have the possibility to be led by the Spirit of God twenty-four hours a day, seven days a week, and the choice to do that is mine. Because I have made a serious decision to follow Jesus for the rest of my life, I consider myself to be one of the sons of God who is led by the Spirit of God as quoted in the verse in the chapter heading. *(Romans 8:14).*

This whole pattern of thinking brings to mind Moses' call to the Israelites, in his very long farewell speech. (Nearly the whole of the book of Deuteronomy!) Moses reminded the wandering people of all that had happened to them, or to their parents, and warned them of the dangers to come. He acknowledged that the Lord was the One who had led them to this point, and was asking them each to choose for themselves to continue to be led by His Spirit.

Deuteronomy 30:19-20 *Now choose life, so that you and your children may live, and that you may love the LORD your God, listen to His voice, and hold fast to Hm. For the LORD is your life ....*

Those who are led by the Spirit are sons of God, and they are those who choose life for themselves and their offspring. Our choices today have very long lasting effects, for ourselves but also the generations to follow. Christians need to live like those who love the Lord, who hear the Lord, and are obedient to His commands. Let's do it together!

* * *

Now let's return to the verse we were analyzing, and look at it more closely.

Romans 8:12-14 *Therefore, brothers,* ***we have an obligation*** *- but it is not to the sinful nature, to live according to it. (Emphasis mine)*

Becoming a Christian is not a magic wand that puts everything in order and makes a person live happily ever after, like a fairy story. It is the first step on a long journey. A journey into life at its very best, a journey towards Heaven, in which from the very beginning, we can get a taste of what is to come at the end. As soon as a new believer dedicates their life to Christ, the whole of the Kingdom of God is available to them. But as Jesus told His disciples, it is too much for us to bear in our present state. In some versions the word "bear" is translated as "understand".

> John 16:12 *"I have much more to say to you, more than you can now bear (understand)."*

Jesus goes on in the following verse to promise His disciples that the Spirit of Truth will lead them into "all truth", and He promises the same for us today. The obligation that Paul talks about in the verse quoted above is to listen to the Spirit of truth, and not listen to our own souls. Paul goes on to explain it further.

> Romans 8:12-14 *Therefore, brothers, we have an obligation-- but it is not to the sinful nature, to live according to it.* ***For if you live according to the sinful nature, you will die; but if by the Spirit you put to death the misdeeds of the body, you will live,*** *(Emphasis mine)*

Thus the obligation is obviously ours. We can no longer blame others for our lives; we make our own choices to live according to God's word. We decide to live following the example of Jesus, and as we do, the Spirit of Truth will lead us into "all truth", the truth about Him, and the truth about ourselves. He will help us put to death the deeds of darkness which have so affected our lives up to that point. He will lead us into life in all its fullness, so that we become Sons of God, as He designed mankind to be.

* * *

> <u>Romans 8:12-14</u> *Therefore, brothers, we have an obligation-but it is not to the sinful nature, to live according to it. For if you live according to the sinful nature, you will die; but if by the Spirit you put to death the misdeeds of the body, you will live,* ***because those who are led by the Spirit of God are sons of God.*** *(Emphasis mine)*

As I reflect on "those who are led by the Spirit", my thoughts inevitably turn to Jesus who was led by the Spirit every moment of His life. However the only time that exact phrase appears in the gospels is just after His baptism when Jesus was led by the Holy Spirit into the desert to be tempted. This may not seem to be the most encouraging of verses, but it is one we are obliged to look at in our study of this subject

> <u>Matthew 4:1</u> *Then Jesus was led by the Spirit into the desert to be tempted by the devil.*

> <u>Luke 4:1-2</u> *Jesus, full of the Holy Spirit, returned from the Jordan and was led by the Spirit in the desert, where for forty days He was tempted by the devil.*

Many Christians can testify that immediately after their baptism they passed through a testing time or a "wilderness experience". If a desert experience was necessary for Jesus then why are we surprised that something similar happens to us? Unfortunately, many of those same Christians do not experience Jesus' victory as we see it in the next part of the story. The gospels tell us that Jesus came out of the desert "in the power of the Spirit" *(Luke 4:14).*

Sons of God can expect to be led into the desert to be tested, but they can also expect to pass the test and be led out in power. Being a follower of Jesus does not mean that life will be easy, but it does mean that it will be in the "power of the Spirit": exciting, interesting and fulfilling.

Remember too that the people of Israel were led by the Holy Spirit in the form of a cloud or a pillar of fire. They were led out of slavery, and eventually into the promised land. There is a promised land for us too; let us allow the Spirit to lead us there, and not waste time on the road or spend too long on the mountain (*Deuteronomy 1:6*). Let us learn our lessons quickly during our wilderness experience, and move on to all that the Lord has for us and for our children.

Paul in his letter to the Galatians assures us, as he does in Romans, that the only way to overcome temptation and the desires of the sinful nature, or the soulish desires of our flesh, is to be led by the Spirit. The verse from Luke chapter 4 quoted above reminds us that Jesus entered the desert, or the place of temptation, "full of the Holy Spirit". If He had not been full of the Spirit, he could not have succeeded in the way He did. The devil tempted Him to take short cuts, and to satisfy the desires of His flesh in just the same way that he tempts us. Jesus came out of the desert in the "power of the Spirit", and we can do the same.

Being led by the Spirit means getting His help to overcome the temptations of the devil. This does not mean living under the law, but rather living in the freedom and the power of the Holy Spirit.

> Galatians 5:16-18 *Live by the Spirit, and you will not gratify the desires of the sinful nature. For the sinful nature desires what is contrary to the Spirit, and the Spirit what is contrary to the sinful nature. They are in conflict with each other, so that you do not do what you want. But if you are led by the Spirit, you are not under law.*

One more important thing to remember is that before Jesus was led into the desert by the Holy Spirit, He had received confirmation of who He was.

> Luke 3:21-22 *Jesus was baptised too. And as He was praying, Heaven was opened and the Holy Spirit descended on Him in bodily form like a dove. And a voice came from Heaven: "You are my Son, whom I love; with You I am well pleased."*

Jesus never had an identity crisis, He knew who He was. Jesus knew where He had come from, He knew where He was going and He knew He was the only Son of the Father. As a divine being He had no problems at all. However, He chose to leave His divinity behind Him and, as a totally human person, He experienced all human emotions including the same insecurities that we feel. One of the reasons He came was to identify with us in our daily lives, in our sufferings, our worries, our nervousness. So He would be just as pleased as you or I would be to receive this confirmation of His true identity.

God will confirm to you too, who you are in Him. It may not be a voice from Heaven that others can hear, but He will reassure you in your moments of doubt. He will tell you that you too are His beloved child and that He is pleased with you, without you doing anything to merit it. At this point in His life, Jesus had done no miracles, nobody knew who He was, He had done nothing to deserve God's approbation, except be baptised, but God was pleased with Him. God is pleased with you too. He may not be pleased with everything you have done to date, but He loves you more than you can possibly understand, and He is pleased with who you are today.

Creation is waiting for those Sons of God who know their Heavenly Father, and know that He is pleased with them, first of all for who they are, and not for what they do. They are those who allow themselves to be led by the Spirit at all times, knowing that that same Holy Spirit will lead them into more and more obedience to Himself, helping them to leave behind all that is not from the Lord. Those who truly seek to be led by the Spirit have the ability to be Sons of God in the same way that Jesus was. He overcame all earthly temptations by the power of the Spirit. We can do that too.

* * *

What does the Bible tell us about where the Spirit will lead those who are willing to be led. This is not a comprehensive list, but it is an encouragement to show what is available to us as sons of God when we allow ourselves to be led by His Spirit.

- Holy Spirit will lead us into the desert, but out again in His power. *(Luke 4)*
- He will lead us into understanding of His will and His word. *(Philippians 3:15)*
- He will lead us out of slavery into freedom. *(Luke 4:18)*
- He will lead us out of the lies we have believed and into His truth. *(John 16:13)*
- He will lead us out of darkness into light. *(Matthew 4:16 & John 8:12)*
- He will lead us out of poverty into prosperity. *(3 John 2 KJV)*
- He will lead us to have peace in all situations. *(John 14:27)*
- He will lead us out of sickness into health. *(1 Peter 2:24)*
- He will lead us out of mourning into joy. *(John 16:20)*
- He will lead us from a cursed life into a blessed one. *(Deuteronomy 28)*

Doesn't that make you want to be a Son of God, led by the Spirit full time? It does me. As you continue through the chapters which follow, be encouraged to move into *ALL* that Jesus has for you.

Chapter 3

The Light Went Out

Way back at the beginning of time, God walked and talked with Adam in the garden of Eden. I wish there was more in the Bible about that time. We have no idea how long Adam and Eve lived in the garden after they were created. We have no accounts of the fun they had together in that perfect place. The Bible jumps very quickly from creation to sin. It is difficult to imagine what it must have been like for the very first Son of God to walk and talk and have fun with his Daddy before anyone else was around. We cannot imagine a world with no sin, no negativeness, no lack, no aggression, no greed, no wars, no worries, which is what both Adam and Eve experienced at the beginning of life in the Garden of Eden.

Because we know that creation is groaning and waiting for the last-days Sons of God, we can imagine that creation rejoiced as Adam walked with God. God looked on all that He had made and it was very good *(Genesis 1:31)*. It was all that He had intended it to be. Everything was in harmony. Have we any idea of what that looked like? Everything Adam learned came directly from God. One of the things His Father told him was not to eat of one certain tree in the middle of the garden; the tree of the knowledge of good and evil, because if he did there would be very serious consequences.

> Genesis 2:16-17 *And the LORD God commanded the man, "You are free to eat from any tree in the garden; but you must not eat from the tree of the knowledge of good and evil, for when you eat of it you will surely die."*

I have often wondered how Adam responded to that instruction. Did he say "No problem boss, whatever you say"? Did he ask what it meant to die? Remember that up to this point nothing had died, so we suppose that Adam had only a theoretical understanding of death. Maybe he didn't even have that. There had only been creation, only beauty, only fun and excitement every day, exploring a beautiful weed-free garden with the amazing Creator. There had been no destruction, no death, no deterioration. Maybe Adam was interested in what 'evil' might be, because up to this moment, he had only experienced good, only perfection, only wonderful things at the hand of his God, his Father, his companion and his very best friend. His only friend!

As long as we live outside of Heaven we will probably never know the truth about Adam's situation, and maybe once we get to Heaven these things will not be important, but they are interesting subjects to think about here, while we are on our journey into the next life.

Whatever the discussion around the tree was, that day in the garden of Eden, Adam had either completely forgotten it or decided to ignore it when Eve offered him the fruit of the forbidden tree. Suddenly it was too late. Suddenly he knew what death meant. Suddenly he had a knowledge of good and evil that he hadn't had before.

Did Adam simply chose to not remember God's instruction? (Do we do that?) or maybe he remembered and talked himself into ignoring what God had said. (Isn't that what we often do too?) Maybe Adam had often walked past that tree in the middle of the garden, and wondered about the mystery. Maybe he was curious and saw the conversation with the serpent as a harmless lesson in enlightenment, opening the door into the mysterious unknown. I believe he had no idea of the enormity of what he was about to do, no idea that one bite of that fruit would not just solve the mystery, but make a contract with Satan that would affect thousands of generations to follow. Those who dabble in other religions, just out of curiosity, have no idea that they too are taking a step that will affect not only their own lives but also those of future generations in their own blood line. How important it is that we are led by the Spirit of God, and not led by the spirit of the enemy.

Let's go back to the garden experience. The question for us, here on the earth and especially in this book, is "what did it mean to die?" God had said that Adam and

Eve would die, and yet their story continues, so they continued to live, at least their bodies did. In modern thought we tend to define death in corporal terms, but what did dying mean in Heaven's terminology? Death is often described as separation from God, and yet when people die in our twenty-first century western Christian communities we see them being reunited with God. Can death have more than one meaning?

One of the ways I like to explain what happened in the garden all those thousands of years ago is: "the light went out!"

Adam was made in God's image with a spirit, a soul, and a body. God is a triune God, so anyone made in His image must also be a three part being. The three manifestations of God referred to in the Bible are the Father, the Son and the Holy Spirit. It is not the purpose of this book to develop that theme, we are concerned here with the three parts of man. Paul refers to these in his first letter to the Thessalonians.

> 1 Thessalonians 5:23 *May your whole spirit, soul and body be kept blameless at the coming of our Lord Jesus Christ.*

In the gospel of John, we are left in no doubt that God is primarily spirit.

> John 4:24 *God is spirit, and His worshippers must worship in spirit and in truth."*

If the spirit part of God is the largest part, one would expect the spirit part of man to be the largest part too. We are made in God's image, remember? The verse from Thessalonians quoted above confirms that thought by mentioning all three parts of a person, but there are other Bible references that I see as confirmation of this theme. We read about John the Baptist being strong in spirit, but have no reference to his physical qualities.

> <u>Luke 1:80</u> *And the child (John the Baptist) grew and became strong in spirit;*

In his second letter to the Corinthians, Paul has a lot to say about daily life and he pleads with the church there to separate themselves from unholy things. He promises the Lord's acceptance as His children if they do so.

> <u>2 Corinthians 7:1</u> *Since we have these promises, dear friends, let us purify ourselves from everything that contaminates body and spirit, perfecting holiness out of reverence for God.*

It is a call for those who call themselves God's people to be Holy, to have large spirits which are in tune with His Spirit. In fact, that is the story of the whole Bible. From the beginning God is calling for a holy nation to be His people. After the exodus from Egypt God told the Israelites "You are to be my holy people" (Exodus 22:31). Later on He told them why.

> <u>Leviticus 11:44</u> *I am the LORD your God; consecrate yourselves and be holy, because I am holy.*

The New Testament message is the same:

> 1 Peter 2:9 *You are a chosen people, a royal priesthood, a holy nation, a people belonging to God.*

We become holy by encouraging our spirits to grow. Let's just take another very brief look at the verse in Thessalonians that speaks of the three parts of man.

> *1 Thessalonians 5:23 May your whole spirit, soul and body be kept blameless at the coming of our Lord Jesus Christ.*

Often in our every day lives the first things on any list are the most important. Let me give you a very simple illustration, and please forgive me if it appears flippant which is not my intent:

If you went to the shop to buy a can of tomato soup, and you read the ingredients on the side of the can, you would expect the first thing in the list to be tomatoes, followed by everything else put in to make the contents good, tasty and long-lasting. I think Paul had the same idea when he told the Thessalonians to take care of their spirit, then their soul, then their body, in that order, the first thing on the list being the biggest, or at least the most important. We will return to this thought later, but for the moment, let's go back to the question we asked earlier. Can death have more than one meaning?

Let us consider the effects of death happening not to the body, but to the spirit.

Adam ate the forbidden fruit, and consequently his spirit died. The first result of that death was that Adam and Eve knew they were naked. Why had they not known this before? Why had they not seen each other before? What had so covered their bodies that they had not been conscious of them? I believe that as Adam's teeth sank into that fruit which was so delicious, as the first drips of juice ran down his chin, his spirit died. Instantly he knew that something terrible had happened. His body felt the first cold clammy sensation anyone had ever experienced as spiritual life left, and spiritual death entered. The light went out.

For Eve too came the same experience of separation from God, and the first couple on the face of the earth looked at each other in horror. They were embarrassed by their own nakedness, their souls were laid bare, the protective "light" of their spirit had disappeared, and they hid from the Lord their maker.

* * *

Let's look a bit closer at that "light" that went out.

When Moses had spent some time in the presence of the Lord, his face glowed with the radiance of His presence, and the children of Israel were so frightened that they asked Moses to cover his face.

> <u>Exodus 34:29-35</u> *When Moses came down from Mount Sinai with the two tablets of the Testimony in his hands, he was not aware that his face was radiant*

because he had spoken with the LORD. When Aaron and all the Israelites saw Moses, his face was radiant, and they were afraid to come near him. But Moses called to them; so Aaron and all the leaders of the community came back to him, and he spoke to them. Afterwards all the Israelites came near him, and he gave them all the commands the LORD had given him on Mount Sinai.

When Moses finished speaking to them, he put a veil over his face. But whenever he entered the LORD's presence to speak with Him, he removed the veil until he came out. And when he came out and told the Israelites what he had been commanded, they saw that his face was radiant. Then Moses would put the veil back over his face until he went in to speak with the LORD.

If Moses' face glowed to such an extent from spending just enough time with the Lord to converse with Him and receive His instructions, how much more must Adam have radiated the glory of the Lord when he lived totally in His presence every minute of the day. When he bit into the fruit of the tree of the knowledge of good and evil, his light went out. The glory of God departed from him, and his spirit died. I see it like this:

Adam was made in three parts; spirit, *(represented by light gray in the picture)* soul, *(represented by black)* and body *(represented by dark gray)*. After eating the fruit, Adam became body and soul with a dead spirit. (The picture below) Work became the curse of mankind and Adam had to work to keep his body alive. His soul, or we could say his fleshly nature, took over the ruling of his life, and there was no more spirit. The light had gone out.

From this point on Adam's main concern became keeping his body alive. No more thought for his spirit which gave no more light.

The best example the Bible gives of a person glowing with the Spirit of God is Jesus on the mountain of transfiguration;

> Matthew 17:1-2 *Jesus took with him Peter, James and John the brother of James, and led them up a high mountain by themselves. There He was transfigured before them. His face shone like the sun, and His clothes became as white as the light.*

Very briefly, and only once that we read about, Jesus allowed the inner circle of disciples to see what He looks like with the light turned on.

I believe when we become Christians the light gets turned back on, and we begin to recover the glow that was lost with Adam's sin. The third diagram shows what happens as we become Christians. Our spirit is born again, and once it is alive and upright once more, it needs feeding and nurturing in the Truth of God's Word. Our goal should be to have our spirits larger than our souls, so that we are in constant connection with the Spirit of God and led by Him every moment of the day.

As a person's spirit grows in the things of God, so that person becomes a son of God who is led by the Spirit of God as quoted in our verse at the beginning of the first chapter *(Romans 8:14)*. But there is a battle. Often our soulish nature has been managing our lives for too long, and it is very reluctant to give up that control. Paul told Timothy to "fight the good fight", and we must do that too.

> 1 Timothy 1:18-19 *Fight the good fight, holding on to faith and a good conscience.*

> 1 Timothy 6:11-12 *But you, man of God, flee from all this* (love of money and earthly wealth), *and pursue righteousness, godliness, faith, love, endurance and gentleness. Fight the good fight of the faith. Take hold of the eternal life to which you were called*

Many Christians are fighting a fight that is not the good one. We learn a little about spiritual warfare and rush off to fight the demons that we see everywhere. Unfortunately, too often in our Christian communities, the first demonic forces we try to fight are in the pastor, others in our church, or other denominations. Paul is telling Timothy, that the most important fight is within himself, to keep his own faith encouraged, to pursue a godly life first for himself, not to go chasing the evil things, real or imagined, in others.

We need to allow our new born spirits to grow in the Lord, before we go off trying to change the world. Yes, we need to encourage ourselves, and yes we need to share our new found life in the Lord with others, but sometimes over-enthusiastic Christians do more harm than good because we haven't really got a grip on what that new life is all about.

Once we have our light switched on again by a new-born spirit, we need to feed it well. In our daily feeding habits, we nourish our bodies with all sorts of different foods, some good, some bad, but most of us try to eat fairly healthily, and most of us know what is good for our body's health and what is not. Our souls and our spirits get fed by the things we see, the things we say, and the things we hear. The nature of the things we focus on either feeds our souls or it feeds our spirits, the choice is ours.

If we watch demonic videos, violent films, listen to the stories of world disasters, get depressed by watching the global news, our souls feed very well, they thrive on those worldly things that may not in themselves be evil, but that do nothing to encourage our spiritual growth.

To make one's spirit grow, a person needs to listen to the Lord, and feed on His Word, on praise and worship music, and watch programmes and films that are not destructive.

The book of proverbs is full of very good advice about living in a way that frees our spirits to live long healthy lives, not in submission to the soulish nature.

> Proverbs 4:20-27 *My son, pay attention to what I say; listen closely to my words. Do not let them out of your sight, keep them within your heart; for they are life to those who find them and health to a man's whole body. Above all else, guard your heart, for it is the wellspring of life. Put away perversity from your mouth; keep corrupt talk far from your lips. Let your eyes look straight ahead, fix your gaze directly before you. Make level paths for your feet and take only ways that are firm. Do not swerve to the right or the left; keep your foot from evil.*

Let us recognise the fight that needs to be fought, let us work on feeding our spirits with God's Word, let us spend time equipping ourselves with everything God provides. Then we will be prepared to "fight the good fight", the right fight, the one specially saved for us by the Lord who has very specific plans for every single one of His children.

I encourage you to take responsibility and make your own spirit grow, remembering that the aim is to be Sons of God, as Jesus was, spirit first, with soul and body following. That is Paul's prayer for the Thessalonians, quoted earlier in this chapter, and copied again below. Let's pray it for ourselves, take care of our spiritual diets, and encourage our lights to shine brightly.

1 Thessalonians 5:23 *May your whole spirit, soul and body be kept blameless at the coming of our Lord Jesus Christ.*

Matthew 5:16 *Let your light shine before men, that they may see your good deeds and praise your Father in Heaven.*

Chapter 4

Sons, Not Daughters

From the beginning you may have noticed that I have not mentioned being a "daughter of God", and I have written of being a "child of God" only a couple of times. Both these expressions have their uses, but the verses which prompted this study *(Romans 8:14-19)* clearly talk about sons and not daughters or children. I am aware that this can be an problem for many readers.

This chapter is an attempt to address the issues of those who are concerned with the rights of women in our modern society. In the majority of cases, it is a good thing to fight for the rights of those who are oppressed, put down, and not treated with honour and respect. However, sometimes good causes can be pushed to an extreme and thus lose their balance. Re-writing the Bible to include words of feminine gender is in my opinion, one of those extremes.

If you, as a woman, have a problem with what God gives to His sons with no apparent mention of daughters, then please ask Him to help you understand. If you are offended by verses that speak to men without mentioning women, then please, ask another believer to pray with you and help you see the truth and balance of God's Word.

Ask the Lord to show you if the offense you are feeling is because you have been hurt by a man, or men, because past hurts can often be the root of such un-biblical ways of thinking. Another cause of an ingrained attitude about male / female issues can be being brought up by a mother who needed to control, or who had been hurt herself because of a man's behaviour in the past, maybe an absent father, an abusive father or another perturbed family member.

If you discover that in your case there has been emotional or physical abuse, then please seek help from someone you can trust. It is not the purpose of this book to delve into healing issues. Remember that Jesus has called us all to be His Bride, that goes for the men too. If the guys can be the Bride then the girls can be Sons.

In Biblical times, the first son was the heir of the family, whatever that meant, rich or poor. Fathers had to make special arrangements for second, third, and subsequent children. In many different ethnic and cultural groups all across the world this practice continues even into the twenty-first century. The eldest son is recognised as the heir, daughters get very little recognition when it comes to inheritance, except for maybe a dowry at the time of their wedding, and not a lot of provision is made for subsequent sons. I am not saying this is right or wrong, just that despite sterling efforts by those who work for equality, it is still a fact of life in much of the world today.

There are Biblical accounts that confirm these ideas about inheritance, and there are Biblical accounts that overturn them. In the story of Jacob and Esau, the older brother sold his birthright to his younger sibling because he was hungry *(Genesis 25:26 and following).* Many sermons have been preached on that story.

Abraham who waited so long to be a father, had Ishmael first, but he was not the child of his wife Sarah, so Abraham sent him away from home, at the request of Sarah, but also with the agreement of God *(Genesis 20:10-14).* It was God's plan that the second son receive the inheritance. Many sermons have been preached on that story too.

Abraham went on to treat Isaac as his first son and heir. After Sarah, the mother of Isaac died, Abraham had six other children, but he still left everything he had to Isaac *(Genesis 25:1-6).*

Whether we like the idea or not, we have to agree that those who wrote the Bible were living in a culture where sons were very important and daughters less so. But the important question is what does God think? Many good books have been written about the importance of women to the Lord, but let us just look here at a couple of verses that have helped clarify the matter for me, and I hope they will for you. We will look first at what the New Testament has to say:

> <u>Galatians 3:27-29</u> *...all of you who were baptised into Christ have clothed yourselves with Christ. There is neither Jew nor Greek, slave nor free, male nor female, for you are all one in Christ Jesus. If you belong to Christ, then you are Abraham's seed, and heirs according to the promise.*

To be clothed with Christ is the important clue here. I cannot say it is something I fully understand, but when we look at someone today, we see their clothes, not their bodies. Often the clothes, or the hairstyles or what we might call "the covering" tells us if a person is male or female. What Paul is saying here, is that our "covering" should say that we are believers, that we are clothed with Him. And if we are clothed with Christ, then nothing else matters.

Often when I travel in the USA people tell me that I look European. Is it because of what I wear, my hairstyle, the way I walk? I don't know, but I have to admit that once out of my own culture, I look European. Sometimes when my husband and I go into Paris with our many visitors, we do some "tourist spotting". Very often we can tell from the "look" of a person which nationality they are. Sometimes it is what they are wearing, sometimes it is facial features, voice, or hairstyles, occasionally we are wrong, but usually we can make a pretty good guess. I long for the day when we can go "Christian spotting".

When we can look at someone and know without a doubt that they are Christians. I am expecting the day to arrive when people stop me in the street, and say "You look like a Christian, tell me about your God."

The Lord promises to make a new nation, a nation of His followers, those who are really the Sons of God that creation recognizes. I am sure that we believers will recognize each other too, and when we do, male, female, clothes, hairstyles, origins will cease to be important. When that happens, we will recognise how often we have wasted our energies fighting a fight which was not the right one.

The last phrase in the Galatians scripture quoted above gives us the reason why male or female, Jew or Greek are not important. It is because we are "heirs according to the promise". The promise is the one that God gave to Abraham all those thousands of years ago. In Jesus we can all become heirs, we can all be the same as the eldest son. God has no favourites.

> Acts 10:34 *"I now realise how true it is that God does not show favoritisme.*

For Him we are all equal. Hallelujah!

> Romans 8:16-17 *The Spirit himself testifies with our spirit that we are God's children. Now if we are children, then we are heirs - heirs of God and co-heirs with Christ,*

Please note that there is no mention of sons or daughters in this verse. When it is important, the Lord ensures that the message is clear. A little further in the same chapter, another verse confirms these thoughts.

> Romans 8:29 *For those God foreknew He also predestined to be conformed to the likeness of his Son, that he might be the firstborn among many brothers.*

Be convinced today that God foreknew you, and predestined you to be conformed to the likeness of His Son, maybe not in bodily form (male or female), but in spirit. In the Spirit, there is neither male nor female. We are all heirs. Become an heir today, and fight the good fight of faith. Dare to declare yourself a Son of the most high God.

* * *

Before we leave this discussion of male and female, I would like to spend a few minutes looking at an interesting story in the Old Testament.

When the children of Israel were finally ready to enter the promised land and to have it shared out among them, the Lord gave very specific instructions to Moses, as He had done all through the desert wanderings. The distribution of the land is recorded for us in the book of Numbers, and I can imagine that Moses must have been very happy to have the Lord supervise the whole thing, what a huge problem of statistics it could have been! It is summed up for us in the following verses:

Numbers 26:52-56 *The LORD said to Moses, "The land is to be allotted to them (the sons in all the families that had just been counted) as an inheritance based on the number of names. To a larger group give a larger inheritance, and to a smaller group a smaller one; each is to receive its inheritance according to the number of those listed. Be sure that the land is distributed by lot. What each group inherits will be according to the names for its ancestral tribe. Each inheritance is to be distributed by lot among the larger and smaller groups."*

It all seemed very clear and organised until the first women's lib group arose and presented their case not just to Moses, but before the whole assembly. What happened is described at the beginning of the next chapter in Numbers.

Numbers 27:1-10 *The daughters of Zelophehad son of Hepher, belonged to the clan of Joseph. The names of the daughters were Mahlah, Noah, Hoglah, Milcah and Tirzah. They approached the entrance to the Tent of Meeting and stood before Moses, Eleazar the priest, the leaders and the whole assembly, and said, "Our father died in the desert. He was not among Korah's followers, who banded together against the LORD, but he died for his own sin and left no sons. Why should our father's name disappear from his clan because he had no son? Give us property among our father's relatives." So Moses brought their case before the LORD and the LORD said to him, "What Zelophehad's daughters are saying is right. You must certainly give them property as an inheritance among their father's relatives and give their father's inheritance over to them. Say to the Israelites, "If a man dies and leaves no son, give his inheritance over to his daughter. If he has no daughter, give his inheritance to his brothers. If he has no brothers, give his inheritance to his father's brothers. If his father had no brothers, give his inheritance to the nearest relative in his clan, that he may possess it.""*

The first women's protest group recorded in the Bible was successful, and the result was a clarifying of inheritance laws for every one else in their nation. Be encouraged that what Paul said in the first verse quoted in this chapter is true. Here it is again:

Galatians 3:28-29 There is neither Jew nor Greek, slave nor free, male nor female, for you are all one in Christ Jesus. If you belong to Christ, then you are Abraham's seed, and heirs according to the promise.

* * *

One thing remains to be discussed before leaving this subject of identity or sexuality. Let us clear up any confusion about homosexuality.

When Paul talks about there being neither male nor female, he does not mean that a person can change from one to the other. Paul makes no allowances at all for anyone having gender issues. In the first chapter of the book of Romans he makes this very clear, and tells us that sexual sins came in because of idolatry.

<u>Romans 1:21-27</u> *For although they knew God, they neither glorified Him as God nor gave thanks to Him, but their thinking became futile and their foolish hearts were darkened. Although they claimed to be wise, they became fools and exchanged the glory of the immortal God for images made to look like mortal man and birds and animals and reptiles.* ***Therefore*** *God gave them over in the sinful desires of their hearts to sexual impurity for the degrading of their bodies with one another. They exchanged the truth of God for a lie, and worshipped and served created things rather than the Creator--who is for ever praised. Amen.* ***Because of this****, God gave them over to shameful lusts. Even their women exchanged natural relations for unnatural ones. In the same way the men also abandoned natural relations with women and were inflamed with lust for one another. Men committed indecent acts with other men, and received in themselves the due penalty for their perversion.* *(Emphasis mine)*

Sexual purity is not just a fad invented by Paul, but an instruction from God. In the book of Genesis chapter 19 we have the account of Sodom and Gomorrah, a story of sexual sin which is referenced many other times throughout the Bible and which has become a legend known today, even among non-believers.

When God gave the law to Israel in the desert, he left no doubts as to what is right and what is wrong. The rules about sexuality were very detailed, and can be read in

Leviticus 18, but for our subject in this book we will just refer to one verse. I do recommend that you read the whole chapter, just to see how specific the Lord was. As you read it, pray for those you know, and those you don't, who have fallen into sexual sin.

> *Leviticus 18:22 Do not lie with a man as one lies with a woman; that is detestable.*

As you read on in Leviticus 18, you will see that the laws tell us that the result of these sexual sins is the defilement of the land. No wonder the nations of the world have problems today; we are all living on defiled land. God is calling intercessors today to walk the land and pray for forgiveness. Many people are travelling under God's specific directions to countries not their own to pray for the land and to plead the redemption of the blood of Jesus shed for the forgiveness of all sins.

Praise God that He is calling His children to move on His behalf.

Sons of God and Heirs of the promise rise up! There is work to be done.

Chapter 5

Sons, Not slaves

It is very important that we understand the difference between sons and slaves. If you have been brought up in a healthy, happy environment, perhaps you won't see the need at first to look into this point deeper. Unfortunately, far too many people have had the experience of a disfunctional family life, or even no family life at all. Many people had parents who mistreated them, seriously abused them, or desired that they act as servants all the time, which is a form of abuse. Those children's idea of being someone's offspring is warped, and not at all as God intended it. We will look into the problems with parenting a little in chapter 8 "*The Good Father*", and in chapter 12 "*Parenting the End-Time Sons of God*".

For the moment let's look at one of the Biblical stories which I believe best illustrates my point.

> <u>Exodus 3:7-8</u> *The LORD said, "I have indeed seen the misery of my people in Egypt. I have heard them crying out because of their slave drivers, and I am concerned about their suffering. So I have come down to rescue them from the hand of the Egyptians and to*

bring them up out of that land into a good and spacious land, a land flowing with milk and honey."

When God spoke to Moses from the burning bush, He first identified Himself, then came quickly to the point saying: "I have seen the misery of **MY** people" *(emphasis mine),* God's children were in slavery and He was going to do something about it. Please note that God's intention was not just to release them from slavery and then leave them to themselves; He was intending to very quickly take them out of Egypt and on into the Promised Land. It can be said that "He brought them out to bring them in". (You might like to compare this idea with the list at the end of chapter one, which talks about being led by the Spirit and where we talked about Jesus being taken into the desert in order to brought out in the power of the Holy Spirit.) Unfortunately the Israelites' lack of faith, (their disobedience and their rebellion) resulted in them spending a very long time trying to reach the promised land.

There are many similarities between these Israelites and Christians today. God brings us out of slavery to the enemy, and wants to bring us into the fullness of being His Sons, but too many of us never get that far. Jesus and Paul both talked about the freedom we have as followers of Christ, but how many of us truly understand that freedom enough to fully embrace it in our daily lives?

John 8:36 *So if the Son sets you free, you will be free indeed.*

2 Corinthians 3:17 *Now the Lord is the Spirit, and where the Spirit of the Lord is, there is freedom.*

Galatians 5:1 *It is for freedom that Christ has set us free. Stand firm, then, and do not let yourselves be burdened again by a yoke of slavery.*

In the last verse referenced here, Paul is quite angry with the church in Galatia because some of their leadership were trying to put them into religious slavery with lots of rules to be followed. Sadly, many churches still do that today. Certain churches insist that if you are a member then you must serve in some form. Every member must take a turn to bring the flowers or be on the welcome committee, or help with children's ministry. Please note that I am not saying this is wrong, and I do fully support the idea of church members participating in the life of the church. However, we need to serve each other as we are led by the Holy Spirit, not as an obligation to follow community rules. In other extreme situations, members must wear certain clothes to church or rather **not** wear certain clothes to church, there are rules about times, days and dates. Ask yourself what it means to have the freedom that Jesus speaks about. He followed nobody's rules but God's, and that was a rule of love.

Matthew 22:37 *Jesus replied: "Love the Lord your God with all your heart and with all your soul and with all your mind. This is the first and greatest commandment."*

Once we understand even a little about loving the Lord, we have a desire to serve in the church. The church becomes family for many believers, especially those who are far from home because of work or studies. The church also becomes family for those from underprivileged backgrounds who have never known a well balanced loving family. Serving the church seems to be a natural and fulfilling way of giving back some of the love received, and that is a good thing.

The problem begins when we find our identity in the service we perform. It is too easy to settle into a position in the church and then think that others, as well as the Lord, appreciate us only for what we are doing. I must re-emphasise what was stated in chapter 2, that God loves you and me just because He loves us and He is God. Jesus had not yet started His ministry when the Heavenly voice told Him and others that He was God's beloved Son. God loves you and Jesus died for you without you serving Him or the church in any position whatsoever.

The Bible talks about works that are prepared in advance for us to do *(Ephesians 2:10),* but it must be understood that this is in the context of Paul's teaching on Grace. We can do nothing to earn God's love, it is just a gift of His Grace.

> *Ephesians 2:8-10 For it is by grace you have been saved, through faith - and this not from yourselves, it is the gift of God - not by works, so that no-one can boast.*

> *For we are God's workmanship, created in Christ Jesus to do good works, which God prepared in advance for us to do.*

According to the end of this quotation, there are works to be done. God has very specific tasks for each one of us, but the most important thing is to first understand His Grace. It is through His Grace that we can become His Sons, inheriting the promises of Abraham.

> Galatians 3:29 *If you belong to Christ, then you are Abraham's seed, and heirs according to the promise.*

The works to be done are for the Sons of God to do: works to be done by those who know Father God, who understand His love for them as well as for all mankind. The things we are called to do are works of love for others, a love inherited from our Heavenly Father. Jesus told His disciples, and those of us who have chosen to believe in Him and follow Him that we would do greater works than He had done *(John 14:12)*. The reason He gives for this is that He is going to the Father, and Paul says later that Jesus is interceding for us there at His Father's side *(Romans 8:34)*.

Do you think Jesus is interceding for you to do good works, or for you to know first of all who you are in Him? I believe His first and repeated prayer for us is that we know the love of the Father and become the Sons we are meant to be. Have you ever studied Paul's prayer for the Ephesians?

<u>Ephesians 3:17-19</u> And I pray that you, being rooted and established in love, may have power, together with all the saints, to grasp how wide and long and high and deep is the love of Christ, and to know this love that surpasses knowledge--that you may be filled to the measure of all the fulness of God.

That's what I believe Jesus is praying for you right now. I can hear Him saying "Father, oh that .... (put your name in here) would grasp the love we have for them! Help them see what it means to be your Son." I think Jesus' prayer for us is that we understand the spirit of adoption, and that each one of us takes our place in His family.

<u>Romans 8:15</u> For you did not receive a spirit that makes you a slave again to fear, but you received the Spirit of sonship. And by him we cry, "Abba, Father."

Paul talks in this verse of those who are slaves to fear. We can have many fears, but too often churchgoers are afraid of not doing enough, or not doing the right thing, of failing themselves, of letting others down, and of disappointing God. The result of these fears is that we constantly do things in order to please. We keep busy, we make ourselves slaves to the jobs that need to be done, or that others think need to be done. I cannot repeat too many times that God loves you and wants you to know the reality of Him being your Heavenly Father before you even begin to find the works He has for you to do.

If you are a worker in the church, or in a Christian community, I urge you to spend some time meditating on what it means to be a Son of your Heavenly Father. You might like to work slowly through the whole of Paul's prayer for the Ephesians. Pray it for yourself today, and take time to let the Father love you. He wants sons not slaves!

> Ephesians 3:14-21 *I kneel before the Father, from whom His whole family in heaven and on earth derives its name. I pray that out of His glorious riches He may strengthen you with power through His Spirit in your inner being, so that Christ may dwell in your hearts through faith. And I pray that you, being rooted and established in love, may have power, together with all the saints, to grasp how wide and long and high and deep is the love of Christ, and to know this love that surpasses knowledge - that you may be filled to the measure of all the fulness of God. Now to Him who is able to do immeasurably more than all we ask or imagine, according to His power that is at work within us, to Him be glory in the church and in Christ Jesus throughout all generations, for ever and ever! Amen.*

In the next chapter of Ephesians, Paul talks about some of the giftings that need to be used in the body of Christ. As you read these verses, note the reason that the gifts are given.

> Ephesians 4:11-12 *It was He who gave some to be apostles, some to be prophets, some to be evangelists, and some*

to be pastors and teachers, to prepare God's people for works of service, so that the body of Christ may be built up.

The body of Christ is made up of people who know Him, think like Him, and act like Him. If the works we do do not accomplish that, then there is a problem somewhere. If we do not know Jesus and His Father intimately, then we cannot lead others to know Him as He wants to be known.

There are other lists of gifts in Romans 12:6-8 and in 1 Corinthians 12, and more can be identified throughout the Bible. It is obviously important that each believer finds their gift, and uses it to bless others and the Lord, but the first and most important instruction we have been given is the first commandment.

Deuteronomy 6:5 *Love the LORD your God with all your heart and with all your soul and with all your strength.*

This is quoted directly by Jesus in three of the four gospels, and the expression "Love the Lord your God" appears six times in the book of Deuteronomy. Moses was obviously trying to get his point across. We must never forget that before God calls us to do anything for Him we must love Him and understand how much He loves us. He wants Sons not slaves.

Between Chapters 5 & 6

In the next four chapters we will look in detail at the story known as "the Prodigal son". This story is copied in full below.

> Luke 15:11-32 *There was a man who had two sons. The younger one said to his father, 'Father, give me my share of the estate.' So he divided his property between them. Not long after that, the younger son got together all he had, set off for a distant country and there squandered his wealth in wild living. After he had spent everything, there was a severe famine in that whole country, and he began to be in need. So he went and hired himself out to a citizen of that country, who sent him to his fields to feed pigs. He longed to fill his stomach with the pods that the pigs were eating, but no-one gave him anything.*
>
> *When he came to his senses, he said, 'How many of my father's hired men have food to spare, and here I am starving to death! I will set out and go back to my father and say to him: Father, I have sinned against heaven and against you. I am no longer worthy to be called your son; make me like one of your hired men.'*

So he got up and went to his father. But while he was still a long way off, his father saw him and was filled with compassion for him; he ran to his son, threw his arms around him and kissed him.

The son said to him, 'Father, I have sinned against heaven and against you. I am no longer worthy to be called your son.' But the father said to his servants, 'Quick! Bring the best robe and put it on him. Put a ring on his finger and sandals on his feet. Bring the fattened calf and kill it. Let's have a feast and celebrate. For this son of mine was dead and is alive again; he was lost and is found.' So they began to celebrate.

Meanwhile, the older son was in the field. When he came near the house, he heard music and dancing. So he called one of the servants and asked him what was going on. 'Your brother has come,' he replied, 'and your father has killed the fattened calf because he has him back safe and sound.'

The older brother became angry and refused to go in. So his father went out and pleaded with him. But he answered his father, 'Look! All these years I've been slaving for you and never disobeyed your orders. Yet you never gave me even a young goat so I could celebrate with my friends. But when this son of yours who has squandered your property with prostitutes comes home, you kill the fattened calf for him!'

'My son,' the father said, 'you are always with me, and everything I have is yours. But we had to celebrate and be glad, because this brother of yours was dead and is alive again; he was lost and is found.'

Chapter 6

The Elder Son

One of the things we must never forget in this story, is that both sons were children of the father. They were very different, had different attitudes, and different life experiences but that did not change the fact that they were sons of the father from the beginning to the end of their lives. In this chapter we will look at the older son.

The Bible doesn't tell us clearly, but we can suppose that the elder brother received his portion of the inheritance as a result of his younger brother's demands for his inheritance. We read very near the beginning of the story that the father divided his goods between the two, but we have no indication that the elder son did anything with what he received. For this son, life continued as it always had. He was working in the field. He had always worked in the field, and he supposed that being a son of his father meant that he worked in the field.

There are many Christians today who think that being a son of the Father means working for him "in the field". Maybe the field is the mission field in a foreign country or maybe it is in the home church, or the local community.

Each of us has a "field" assigned to us by the Father, and I am pleased to say that many of us are faithful workers in that field. Sadly, many of us act as though that is all the Christian life entails; all we can see and think about is "the field". We invest all our time, our energy and our thoughts towards making our field productive. In fact, what happens is that we become a slave to the work which we believe the Father has assigned to us. We never ask for a raise in our wages, we never ask for a day off. We just continue as we always have, working in the field.

In many cases too, although it is not a part of this story, many of us are working in the wrong field. We are doing what we think we should do, or we are doing what others think we should do, and we have not taken time with the Father to find out exactly what it is that He wants us to do.

The first son was resentful of the second son. We suppose this resentment and rejection of his brother happened when the younger one left to see the world, but it is possible that it began long before that. As brothers we can suppose that they had discussed their interests, and their work, but it doesn't take too much imagination to see that they were totally different characters. The first was satisfied with his life, had no wish to see what the rest of the world was like, he was secure in who he was as a son of his father, and probably thought the young one a fool to take so much interest in other things, to even consider travelling to unknown and possibly dangerous places. We can imagine that, like Joseph's brothers, this elder son dismissed his younger sibling as a dreamer.

There is nothing wrong with being satisfied with one's lot, in fact the Bible tells us that this is a gift from God.

(Ecclesiastes 5:19 to accept his lot and be happy in his work - this is a gift of God.)

The problem arises when the happy one expects everyone else to be happy with the same things, and resents people who are different. One who thinks that everything should be done their way, or that others should be like them, is in fact making an idol of himself or herself and is denying the enormous variety of design that our God has created.

How sad it is when families, like the one in this story, are divided. Unfortunately this has been happening since the beginning of time, so why are we surprised? When there were only two brothers on the earth, one killed the other because of anger and jealousy *(Genesis 4)*. Later in the Bible we read of the totally different personalities of Jacob and Esau which led to family strife *(Genesis 27)*. Later still we have the account of the jealousies that caused Joseph's brothers to try to kill him, then sell him as a slave, and lie to his father about what had happened *(Genesis 37)*.

The psalmist was making an important point when he wrote the following:

Psalm 133:1-3 How good and pleasant it is when brothers live together in unity! It is like precious oil poured on the head, running down on the beard, running down on Aaron's beard, down upon the collar of his robes. It is as if the dew of Hermon were falling on Mount Zion. For there the LORD bestows his blessing, even life for evermore.

Jesus instructs us to love one another. Love between brothers is not a feeling it is a choice, a choice to obey the Lord's commandment. It is the same within the church as it is in our home family situations, we must make the decision to love our fellow believers.

* * *

The elder brother in our story saw only the wrong things his brother had done and could not rejoice that the wayward one had come home. He could not forget the work that the younger one had missed doing at home, maybe some of the work had fallen to him as a consequence of his brother's departure. Whatever the reason for his anger, he could not bring himself to forgive.

As Christians, do we rejoice spontaneously when the lost are found, when the wayward come humbly back to the Father? Most of us know we should do that, but in our heart of hearts is there something that says "they don't deserve it"? Is there a feeling that people who have gone so far away, who have misused God's goodness and His gifts, should not be allowed back into the family home?

Do we tell God that these people don't deserve His forgiveness?

It is my experience that many, but by no means all, of the most successful workers in the kingdom today are those who have been a very long way from the church for much of their lives. People who have been involved in witchcraft, drugs, or demonic dealings of any kind find forgiveness through Jesus and then work for Him with all that they have. It seems to me that these people understand the power of the Holy Spirit and the risen Lord, because they have experienced first hand the powers of darkness.

I believe the elder son in our story had had a "middle of the road" sort of life, comfortable, secure, regular income, not too much stress, and he had become complacent, and totally insensitive to anyone in any other situation. The elder brother was offended by the celebration party given for the returned prodigal, he did not think the homecoming was a reason to celebrate. He got angry with the father for rejoicing that the lost son was found. Suddenly out of his anger came resentment that he probably didn't even know was there, and he lists for his father all the things that he had not received, forgetting that he had never once asked for them.

As Christians, we know our heavenly Father has so much for us, but do we pursue those things? Do we ask for what is ours by spiritual inheritance? God didn't leave the asking to us because He wanted to deprive us and see us pleading with Him; He did it because He wanted a relationship with each one of us. When we go to Him to ask for things, He is pleased, but when we ask out of a loving relationship, He is much more satisfied.

Would this son really have been happy to see his younger brother punished for the hurt he had caused? Did he want to see his brother whipped, or sent to work with the animals? Would his anger have been satisfied if he had heard his father tell the wayward one "Son you shouldn't have done what you did, you upset us all, you left work to be done on the farm, your elder brother has had to do twice as much because you left. Now you must be punished for the hurt you have caused us"? Did the elder brother have no understanding at all of forgiveness?

The Christian represented by the older brother here gets very upset when people who have lived a life of sin, who have been far from God, who have had a blasphemous life style, do an about-turn and begin living for the Lord. They think that these people should be made to live in constant regret of the wasted years. How sad!

There are Christians who become upset when someone moves as it were, from the back row of the church to the front row, and becomes very involved. How sad! There are Christians who don't like parties, or maybe they only like their own sort of party, with their own friends, one that they themselves organize. These Christian refuse to go to impromptu celebrations. They can't abide surprises, especially if they are not in control of the situation. What a party they have missed. How sad!

The older brother never left the father's house, he lived with his father all his life, but did he actually have a relationship with him? Many Christians live in the Father's house, or spend a lot of time there, but do they have a real relationship with Him? Many of you reading this book will know what it is like to live with someone and never really know them. Sadly after years of marriage, people can still say, "He (or she) never understood me." Others can say "I never really knew them." Children leave home and declare that their parents have never understood them. The older son in this story, did not feel that his father understood him or cared for him.

This older brother felt badly treated by his father, but who was at fault here? Had this first child ever taken the time to get to know his father, the one who gave him life, the one who had provided all his security as a boy, and later as an adult? We suppose that this father and son had a working relationship, but at home there was nothing in common, no laughter, no fun, no relaxing together.

This older son had worked. He had worked so much that he considered himself a slave: *"All these years I've been slaving for you and never disobeyed your orders."* Do you know believers like that? Do you know people who feel they have spent their lives working for the Lord, never disobeying a letter of the law, and yet feel He has never answered their prayers?

This older brother knew he had an inheritance. The Bible tells us that the father divided his property between his sons *(Luke 15:12)*, but did he think he only had the right to use it after his father had passed away, or retired, or maybe when he himself got married or reached a certain age? Or maybe it was that he preferred to leave it in the bank until later. How many Christians know they have eternal life in Jesus' name, but think that only means getting to Heaven when they die? How many people who have become Christians continue their lives just as before, without tapping into any of the excitement that God has for them?

Remembering the images used in the 3rd chapter, I think these sorts of Christians look like this.

They have a spirit renewed by the saving grace of Jesus, but they have put that spirit in a box. There is no expectation that the spirit will grow, they feed it a little Bible verse each day (a starvation diet!), and just expect it to stay as it is until eternity, which they believe begins after they die. But eternity began before time was created, and it will continue forever. Such a concept is too big for us to grasp completely, suffice it to say that for us as believers we can live in eternity now. Jesus alludes to this in His prayer for believers before going to His death.

> John 17:3 *Now this is eternal life: that they may know You, the only true God, and Jesus Christ, whom You have sent.*

> Ecclesiastes 3:11 *God has made everything beautiful in its time. He has also set eternity in the hearts of men; yet they cannot fathom what God has done from beginning to end.*

Eternal life means knowing God, not just knowing about Him. Being born again is only the beginning of a wonderful relationship which grows and intensifies as a person's spirit grows; this happens when they feed on the word of God and encourage themselves in Him.

Sadly, there is no record of reconciliation between the brothers or between the elder brother and his father. This man chose to take offense, to miss the celebration, and to miss out on his inheritance. Although he remained a son of the father, and continued to work for him, he gained nothing from the relationship. He never had a moment of intimacy with the one who loved him the most. Will he be one of whom Jesus says *"I never knew you" (Matthew 7:23)*?

Chapter 7

The Younger Son

The younger son in our story is very different to his older brother. Here we have the adventurer, the independent one, the one who wants to travel the world and do his own thing. The one who is very aware that his father is rich.

As soon as he was old enough, this son asked for what he knew was his by right and consequently left the paternal home. Do you know Christians who have taken what God has given them, and gone off to live with it in their own way? They have not understood that to use God's gifts wisely they have to live closely with the Father. It is only in staying by His side that we can have the wisdom and intelligence to handle all that He has given us, as well as acquire all He wants to give us in the future. These Christians have ignored the scriptures which encourage us to live not by our own understanding, but by His.

<u>Proverbs 3:1-2 & 5-6</u> *My son, do not forget my teaching, but keep my commands in your heart, for they will prolong your life many years and bring you*

prosperity.
Trust in the LORD with all your heart and lean not on your own understanding; in all your ways acknowledge Him, and He will make your paths straight.

Matthew 11:28-30 *"Come to Me, all you who are weary and burdened, and I will give you rest. Take My yoke upon you and learn from Me, for I am gentle and humble in heart, and you will find rest for your souls. For My yoke is easy and My burden is light."*

As I copy that verse, I am aware of how often I have quoted part of it and not all of it. I know I am not alone in that. Many people can be heard to quote *"My yoke is easy and My burden is light"* but they forget the part just before where Jesus says to learn from Him. As I read it and write it today, I see the importance of the instruction to do just that, to learn from Him. That is what both sons needed to know. How sad that so many people have a resistance to learning from their parents, or from anyone of an older generation. How sad that so many people have a resistance to learning from God! The rebellion of the young is not a modern day problem, it has been around ever since time began, or at least since Eve listened to the serpent and not to Father God.

Let us focus on the fact that the Lord's burden, that is the thing that He gives us to do, is light. I have often been saddened to see Christians and whole church communities who are tired and weary with the work of the Lord, or the work they believe the Lord asked them to do. God does not want us to wear ourselves out with His work. He wants us to rejoice, be happy and get a lot of personal satisfaction and fulfillment out of what we do for Him. Sometimes we are called to carry heavy burdens, but for most of us that is only for a short while. I know there are certain "chosen Sons" who have to carry out extremely difficult tasks, but even they will tell you that there is great joy in doing what the Lord has called you to do.

If the burden you are carrying and the tiredness you are feeling have continued for a long time, maybe it is time to stop. Maybe it is time to seek serious prayer from a wise believer who will help you hear from the Lord. Maybe it is time to put the first commandment first, and remember that the only thing the Lord requires of us is to love Him. Everything else stems from that. If the Lord asks us to carry heavy burdens, He is very quick to assure us of His presence at our side. Being yoked with Him means He takes more than His share of the weight. We need to learn from Him and remember that Jesus only did what He saw the Father doing. If the younger son in Luke chapter fifteen had done that, he would never have left home. He had no understanding of how easy life was because the father was there. But he was soon to find out and to regret his independent spirit.

This younger son in our story went off with all his possessions, with all the father had given him, and he found companions that the father would not have chosen or approved of. He wasted his inheritance, and ended up tired, hungry, thirsty, and helpless. What a pity that he hadn't heeded the advice from the scriptures.

> <u>Proverbs 2:1-6 & 12-16</u> *My son, if you accept my words and store up my commands within you, turning your ear to wisdom and applying your heart to understanding, and if you call out for insight and cry aloud for understanding, and if you look for it as for silver and search for it as for hidden treasure, then you will understand the fear of the LORD and find the knowledge of God. For the LORD gives wisdom, and from His mouth come knowledge and understanding. Wisdom will save you from the ways of wicked men, from men whose words are perverse, who leave the straight paths to walk in dark ways, who delight in doing wrong and rejoice in the perverseness of evil, whose paths are crooked and who are devious in their ways. It will save you also from the adulteress, from the wayward wife with her seductive words.*

Alone in an evil world, far from the advice of his father, the younger son fell prey to the people the Bible warns against. There is a danger in going too far from the family home, there is a danger in going away from the church. The Bible is clear that we should meet together as believers.

<u>Hebrews 10:25</u> *Let us not give up meeting together, as some are in the habit of doing, but let us encourage one another...*

Many people have been hurt by the church and have decided to abandon regular services, to just stay home and pray alone. I don't believe this is wise. It is Satan who brings division, Satan who separates, who calls us to "do our own thing" and be independent. God is the Father of families, and while each of us needs to develop our own character, the best and safest way to do that is within a family situation. The church is meant to be a family.

It doesn't matter which denomination you choose, as long as it is a Bible-based believing church. It doesn't matter which house meetings or prayer meetings you attend. It does not matter where you find your Christian fellowship, but you need to find these things somewhere. We all need to be encouraged by other believers, and we all have a duty to encourage others too. Solitude is not generally part of God's plan. Yes, He often calls us to retreat with Him alone for a limited period of time, but that is so that we can be strengthened, and prepared for the next part of our journey with Him.

The younger son, on his journey through independence, suffered greatly from solitude. The people who claimed to be his friends while he had money, showed their true colours once he had lost everything. He was very hungry, very thirsty, and he ended up with only the pigs to talk to. Then one day he awoke to reality, or at least he realized that the reality he was living might not be the one he was meant to be experiencing. He remembered that life hadn't been so bad when he was at home where he belonged, close to his father, so he made the difficult decision to return.

We don't know how far from home he was when he was feeding the pigs, but we do know that it was "a far country", so I can imagine that he had plenty of time to reflect on things as he walked the long road home. I can imagine the conversations he would rehearse in his mind with each step of the way. I can also imagine that the devil joined in quite regularly with those discussions going on in his mind.

"You've completely blown it!"

"What makes you think your father will take you back in the state you are in?"

"Maybe your father won't even recognize you, you look such a mess!"

"Why should he take you back after all you have done?"

"He probably won't even give you a job."

"That's the only thing left for you now, to work for him"

"But don't expect any wages, you already took what was yours, remember!"

"Maybe if you work hard enough..."

The nearer the repentant son got to home, the more nervous he must have felt, but his father was waiting and watching, and the reception was nothing like he imagined. His loving father who had never given up hope, said: "Welcome back to where you belong. We are stopping work in order to celebrate your return." Many Christians need to hear today that the Heavenly Father doesn't want them to work for Him, but just to be with Him. Maybe He is saying to you right now: "Stop doing things, and just come and enjoy the party with Me."

Christians who have left the Father's side and gone off into the world to live as they chose need to hear this story. They need to know that being a son of the Father doesn't mean fitting into a mold, or living a life of rules with lots of "do not touch" instructions. Living with the Father means celebration, it means forgiveness, it means security and it means love, unending unconditional love.

It is true that Father God has work for us to do, but before we get into a spirit of slavery, we need to understand what it means to be His son, to understand the depths of His love for us. How many times did the Lord say to the children of Israel, "Love the Lord your God with all your heart, all your mind and all your strength"? So many of us love the Lord with a part of our heart, very little of our minds, and use all our strength to serve the church. That is not at all what the Father wants, but we'll look further into the father's attitude in the next chapter.

Both the elder and the younger son needed to learn from their father, not just how to run the estate and how to work on the farm, but they needed to learn about relationships, responsibility and how to be a family. Learning is not only about education and schooling, it is also about life skills. It is about experiencing life, and the best way to do that is in the security of the Father's home.

It is never too late for those of us who have not had secure, well-balanced families to learn about life skills and love. That is what the church is designed to do. In many churches you will find people with a calling for parenting others, to help new believers, and also the not so new believers, overcome the obstacles of a difficult past, and to help them find in Father God the love that they haven't experienced.

When the wayward son returned home, he found the offer of acceptance still open. He found a loving generous father. I think the son receiving the gifts of the father represents a third type of Christian. This is a relationship we will look at more closely in chapter nine.

Chapter 8

The Good Father

When I was a child the story we are looking at in Luke fifteen was always called "The Prodigal Son", more recently it has been referred to as "The story of the Two Sons", but I would prefer to call it "The Good Father". Let's look more closely at the role the father played in all that happened.

The opening line of the story tells us that the man had two sons. That is the only real fact that Jesus gives as He narrates the story. We are left to judge the father's character by his reaction to the circumstances as they are told. As the narration continues we recognize that the father was certainly not poor, that he had a reasonable inheritance to leave for his children. We hear that he had "an estate", enough land to employ them both, and there were well fed servants ready to do his will. We might even call him rich.

When the second son asked for his share in the family business the father never objected, just gave what the son asked, and let him go. How hard that must have been. We can imagine that the Father had been training the son for years, had been trying to teach him about life, but had always been aware of his rebellious spirit, of his need to go off and do his own thing. Maybe when the son finally said: "I'm old enough now to move away from home, give me my inheritance and I'll go and see the rest of the world", the father succumbed without voicing an objection, knowing he just had to allow the son to learn the lessons of life for himself. But how his father's heart must have grieved internally. How he must have prayed for his son's return.

Father God watches sadly as His children wander off His path, leave the security of His family to go and experience the world, and just like the father in the story, God watches constantly for our return. He longs to have His children return to Him. The repetitive cry of the Old Testament prophets was to the people of Israel to turn back to God and leave their rebellious ways. Let's read some of those verses which could have been speaking to this wayward son, calling him to return to his forgiving father.

> Joel 2:13 *Rend your heart and not your garments. Return to the LORD your God, for He is gracious and compassionate, slow to anger and abounding in love, and He relents from sending calamity.*

> Zechariah 1:3 *'Return to me,' declares the LORD Almighty, 'and I will return to you.'*

Jeremiah 3:12 'Return, faithless Israel,' declares the LORD, 'I will frown on you no longer, for I am merciful,' declares the LORD,

Jeremiah 24:7 I will give them a heart to know Me, that I am the LORD. They will be My people, and I will be their God, for they will return to Me with all their heart.

That last verse is a wonderful prophecy still waiting to be fulfilled. The Lord has never stopped calling us to return to Him with ALL OUR HEARTS. The first commandment is still the first commandment. God wants us to love Him with all our mind, heart, soul and strength. Creation is waiting for those who will do that and consequently change the world.

The Father in Luke 15 loved his son unconditionally, just as Father God loves us. He watched constantly for the return of his wayward son, just as the Lord watches for us. As soon as the father saw that the son was on his way back he was "filled with compassion" in the same way that God is for us, and long before the son arrived back home, the father was running to meet him, just as the Lord does for us. He prepared a feast, clothed his son in the best robe, gave him a ring and fresh sandals for his feet. All these things have important spiritual meanings and we will look at them in detail in the next chapter.

I would have liked to call this chapter "The Perfect Father", but there is only one perfect father and that is God, so the Lord would not allow me to do that, but I have to say that I think this father is as good as they get. Few of us would divide our inheritance between our children without at least giving some good advice. Few of us would let our son go off travelling without comment, or voicing our regrets. None of us have had a perfect earthly father, but we do have a perfect heavenly Father who loves us, watches over us in our wayward and rebellious moments, and waits longingly for our return to Him.

Our heavenly Father welcomes us with open arms just as this earthly father did. Please note that there was no reprimand and no criticism. The father did not say: "Oh son, you smell awful, you've been working with pigs, go take a shower and then I'll give you a hug". The father did not say: "I'll give you new clothes to wear, but you can't put them on until you are cleaned up a bit". The father fell on his son's neck and kissed him, can you feel his love as you meditate on that image?

There was never any suggestion that the son had used up his inheritance and now had to work for his living. In fact, even though the father had "divided his property between them" there is no indication in the story that there was a shortage or that there was nothing left to share. So it is with our God; He has more for us in every way than we can imagine. No matter how much you have already received from Him, there is always more, His supplies never run out.

The older son was not happy about the home-coming party as we have already seen in chapter 5, but the Bible tells us that "the father went out and pleaded with him". God wants all His children to enjoy the party, He wants all of us to rejoice over one sinner who repents and returns to Him. They have a party in Heaven when that happens, so should we. *(Luke 15:10)*

Many Christians think of repentant sinners as being those who have been addicts, paedophiles, bank robbers, prostitutes and the like, but in fact each time we draw nearer to God and let a bit more of our fleshly desires be laid at the cross, then there is rejoicing in Heaven. I have said it before, but it is worth repeating: God wants us to love Him with **All** our heart, **All** our mind, **All** our soul and **All** our strength. That's what creation is waiting for. Most of us are a long way from that goal, but let us praise God that He loves us anyway and like this earthly father in our story, He keeps watching for us along the road we have chosen to walk, and He is running towards us as we limp slowly nearer to Him.

It is sad that it takes many of us a long time to "come home" to Father God. We get delayed along the way by all sorts of hindrances, and once we have become Christians we still carry a lot of the effects of our past sins or our physical inheritance with us. Because of this, I want to look at one last Bible reference which I believe speaks multitudes to us about Father God and our relationship with Him.

> John 1:12-13 *Yet to all who received Him, to those who believed in His name, He gave the right to become children of God;- children born not of natural descent, nor of human decision or a husband's will, but born of God.*

Imagine for a moment your family tree. Even if you don't know who your parents were, still they existed and can be there in the genealogical plan in your mind. From those parents and grandparents, for as many generations as you care to remember, you inherited certain things. You probably received good things as well as bad things. Maybe you inherited your looks, the shape of your body, your colouring, your talents, your abilities. Maybe you also had passed down to you a certain sickness that you can see as recurring in your family line. Maybe there are curses or blessings which have come down to you because of decisions made by those who went before you. (To learn more on this subject Deuteronomy 28 makes a very good study.)

Now I suggest you go back and read the verses above again *(John 1:12-13)*, and imagine being adopted by God. What the Lord is saying is that you don't have to inherit any of the bad things from your natural parents. It is as though He cuts you off from that genealogical line and grafts you into His family tree. In that line there are no curses, no problems handed down from generation to generation. Once you are a child of God there are no inherited diseases, only good things come down to you from your Heavenly Father who loves you beyond measure. Isn't that worth a celebration?

Chapter 9

The End Time Son

Let's begin this chapter by remembering the Bible account of the last part of the story. You will remember that I am treating the second son, the one that has been known for years as "the prodigal son" or "the lost son", as a third person once he is headed for home. He is the repentant one who in the end receives everything the father has always wanted to give him. Unfortunately he had to find himself in the depths of despair in order to understand that his father loved him. Even at his return he didn't have very high hopes for his future, expecting to at best be a hired servant. This however is not what happened. His loving, forgiving father welcomed him, blessed him and showered a multitude of blessings on him. When will we as the church today realize that our Father God doesn't want servants, He wants Sons?

> <u>Luke 15:21-24</u> *The son said to him, "Father, I have sinned against heaven and against you. I am no longer worthy to be called your son." But the father said to his servants, "Quick! Bring the best robe and put it on him. Put a ring on his finger and sandals on his*

> *feet. Bring the fattened calf and kill it. Let's have a feast and celebrate. For this son of mine was dead and is alive again; he was lost and is found." So they began to celebrate.*

I will repeat the question. When will we as the church today realize that our Father God doesn't want servants He wants Sons? Once the repentant son returned home he began to truly understand and to receive what was available for him in his father's house. All that the devil had thrown at him during the long slow walk back to where he belonged was to no avail. The father knew better, and gave him a welcome that was beyond his wildest dreams. He also gave him several significant presents. The robe, the ring, the sandals and the feast where they ate the fattened calf. Lets look at what those things can mean for us as the long awaited Sons of God in the last days. I believe accepting those gifts and all that they represent can change us from sons of God (with a small "s") to the Sons of God for whom creation is waiting.

* * *

The Robe

The father called for the best robe for his son, not just a clean robe, or new robe, but the **best** one. Nothing was too good for this forgiven sinner. If he remembered any scripture verses at all, he may well have thought of Isaiah rejoicing in praise to God.

Isaiah 61:10 I delight greatly in the LORD; my soul rejoices in my God. For he has clothed me with garments of salvation and arrayed me in a robe of righteousness, as a bridegroom adorns his head like a priest, and as a bride adorns herself with her jewels.

This is a prophetic verse about the time when the church will really become the Bride of Christ. In the letter to Laodicea *(Revelation 3:18),* we read of Jesus encouraging people to buy from Him white robes to wear, and later in the same book *(Revelation 6:11),* we read of the martyrs being given white robes to wear. The white robes represent the righteousness that Jesus gained for us on the cross, we do nothing to earn them, we only have to believe in Him. He takes off our filthy rags, and dresses us in fine linen. He removes from us all the stains of the world, and gives us clean garments of righteousness to wear. His righteousness.

I like to call the repentant son in our story the third son, because he seems to be a totally different character to the other two, and he is the one who finally, unreservedly accepted what the father had to give. Once we repent of our sins and receive Jesus Christ as our Saviour, then we are a new creation *(2 Corinthians 5:17).* That's what this repentant sinner became. He was given a new robe to wear, a robe that represented the father's forgiveness. It also represented the father's reinstatement of his son in a place of authority in his household.

When Joseph was elevated to a high position in the court of Pharaoh, he was given robes of fine linen to wear *(Genesis 41:42)*. The giving of fine linen was a symbolic action where a person in higher authority, in this case Pharaoh, bestowed honour, respect and authority onto the receiver.

We read about another robe of honour in the story of Esther. When Haman was asked how he thought the king should honour someone who had pleased him, Haman's totally self centred response was to suggest the person be given a robe which had been worn by the king *(Esther 6:8)*.

The robe given to this "third" son would probably have been one his father had worn, and it was given to honour the son who had made the decision to come home, back to his father, to live close to him once more. For the Sons of God awaited by creation this is a wonderful image of Father God honouring them and giving them a robe of righteousness worn by Jesus. It is a picture of acceptance, honour, love, authority and trust.

Another image related to clothing is given in the book of Exodus where God gave Moses very detailed instructions about the priestly garments.

> <u>Exodus 28:3-5</u> *Tell all the skilled men to whom I have given wisdom in such matters that they are to make garments for Aaron, for his consecration, so that he may serve Me as priest. These are the garments they are to make: a breast-piece, an ephod, a robe, a woven*

tunic, a turban and a sash. They are to make these sacred garments for your brother Aaron and his sons, so that they may serve me as priests. Make them use gold, and blue, purple and scarlet yarn, and fine linen.

Accepting a robe from Father God means becoming a priest to serve Him. This robe made for Aaron represented consecration and holiness. It was not something to be taken lightly but was an extremely serious matter in the days when only those of Aaron's line were called to be priests. Because of what Jesus did on the cross for us, we are now all called to be priests to serve our God *(Revelation 1:6)*, and we all have the possibility to put on that robe of righteousness mentioned in Isaiah 61 and described above.

One last verse from Isaiah merits a brief mention before we leave the subject of the robe.

Isaiah 22:21 I will clothe him with your robe and fasten your sash around him and hand your authority over to him. He will be a father to those who live in Jerusalem and to the house of Judah.

This verse makes me think of the vision of Jesus which John describes *(Revelation 1:16)*, where we see Jesus robed in white, wearing a sash and with the double edged sword coming from his mouth. In fact, Isaiah is prophesying the coming of Jesus in glory and authority, and when Jesus told the story of the prodigal son in Luke 15, He was reminding His listeners of the blessings, and the importance of the robe. Those who become real Sons of God, those awaited by creation, have the right to put on the spiritual robe of holiness, acceptance and authority given by Father God.

* * *

The Ring

In the same way that the robe represented an acceptance and an authority given by a higher authority, the ring confirms that authority. In most cultures of the world today a ring is a sign of a covenant or an engagement, it is a sign of love and acceptance. In the story we are looking at, it is no different. The father gave his son a ring, a family ring to show he was accepted back into the family he had once rejected and run away from.

In the story of Joseph, we have already mentioned the robe given by Pharaoh, let's read the full verse here:

> Genesis 41:42 *Then Pharaoh took his signet ring from his finger and put it on Joseph's finger. He dressed him in robes of fine linen and put a gold chain around his neck.*

The highest authority in the land gave Joseph the signet ring off his own finger. When the Bible gives us very specific details, it is because those details are important. It is not just any ring, but his own ring that Pharaoh gives to his ex-prisoner, a ring bearing his own initials, the ring he had already personally used to sign and validate many official documents. He was giving "all authority" to Joseph, just as Father God gave all authority to Jesus centuries later, and as Jesus gave it to His disciples at the end of His own earthly ministry *(Matthew 28:18-19).*

Those who know that they are Sons of God have an understanding of that authority. An authority to seal things with the signet ring of the Father.

As it was with the robe, the image of the ring's authority is repeated in the story of Esther. The king first gave the ring to Haman, then after Haman misused that authority the king retrieved the ring and presented it to Mordecai. In both cases it represented the highest authority in the land. The one who wears the king's signet ring can sign official documents in the name of the king; he is the representative of the one whose ring he bears. As Sons of God, we must remember the story of Haman and never let pride get in the way. If we misuse the gifts the Lord gives us, we will suffer the consequences.

As Christians we are called to be God's representatives in the earth: we have His authority. Jesus gave us His name to use. Creation is waiting for the Sons of God to rise up and move in the authority that He has given us. This is a daunting task, not to be taken lightly. How amazing that the God who created the universe would even think of giving to His subjects the authority to rule His world. It is incomprehensible that the Lord of Heaven and earth would give ruler-ship to those who crucified

His Son! What a gift and what a responsibility. It is time for us to move into that authority in humble obedience recognizing all that we have in the name of Jesus.

* * *

The Sandals

I can imagine that the sandals worn by the son who had worked with the pigs were very messy. They had taken him across many miles, and must have been dirty and worn out. Maybe by the time he arrived home he was walking barefoot because the sandals had been left by the wayside as useless. It would be natural that the father would give him replacements. But there is also an important spiritual significance in the giving of the sandals.

> Ruth 4:7-8 *Now in earlier times in Israel, for the redemption and transfer of property to become final, one party took off his sandal and gave it to the other. This was the method of legalising transactions in Israel. So the kinsman-redeemer said to Boaz, "Buy it yourself." And he removed his sandal.*

The giving or exchange of sandals represented ownership of the land. In the story of the repentant son who returned home the Father was reinstating him as an inheritor of the land. Was he also elevating him over the elder brother who refused to be part of the party? We don't know. What we do know is that the Father did not say: "Sorry son you lost it when you took your share of the family fortune and left home." What a lesson in forgiveness that many church families need to learn.

Another verse which mentions sandals and has an entirely different significance is found in Moses' discourse with the Israelites, the summary of the promised land experiences.

> Deuteronomy 29:5 *During the forty years that I led you through the desert, your clothes did not wear out, nor did the sandals on your feet.*

I love the way the Lord emphasizes things. He could just as easily have said "your clothes and shoes didn't wear out", but Moses, speaking for the Lord, was very specific; "the sandals on your feet"! Where else would you wear sandals I ask myself, but the seemingly unnecessary words are for a specific purpose. God is reminding them that they had walked for 40 years, and still wore the same sandals with which they had started out. It had to be miraculous, and He wanted them to appreciate that when they walk with Him miracles happen. Miraculous provision or miraculous protection of everything they needed all along the way.

In the story of the father and his sons, the sandals represent ownership of the land, as we learned from the book of Ruth, but this gift would also be a reminder for any Jew who knew his scriptures, and most of them did, that their forefathers had walked with the Lord through the desert in just one pair of sandals. Walking with the

Perfect Father brings miracles into being. Are you ready to put on the shoes He wants you to wear and to walk with Him?

* * *

The Fattened Calf

When I was young, I remember hearing the expression "They killed the fatted calf" when referring to a celebration; it is a saying that has made its way into modern day English because of this story. Reading between the lines we can imagine that the calf was ready and prepared for such a time as this. The father was ready for his son's return, and the servants did not need any explanation as to which calf they were to kill and prepare for the feast. They had been witnesses to the father's preparations, to his faith that his son would one day come home again.

In Heaven a celebration banquet is being prepared in faith that the "lost sons" will return home to Father God.

> Revelation 19:7 *Let us rejoice and be glad and give him glory! For the wedding of the Lamb has come, and His bride has made herself ready.*

The bride is the church, the bride is made up of believers who love the Lord with all their heart, mind, soul and strength. We are in the process of making ourselves ready as we draw closer to Him each day, as we learn to live as real Sons of God, as we understand what is our real inheritance just as the repentant son discovered in the story of Luke chapter fifteen. Let's do it together!

Chapter 10

The Model - Jesus

> Romans 8:19 *The creation waits in eager expectation for the Sons of God to be revealed.*

Creation has been waiting for Sons of God who are just like Jesus. We ask again: who are these Sons of God? We have seen in chapters six and seven that neither of those Biblical models of sons from Luke fifteen were exactly what the Perfect Father wants. Let us now look at the model that Father God gave us in Jesus. Who was He? What was He like? Who did He say He was? And the biggest question of all, how can we become like Him?

In answer to the first question, "who was He?", we can of course reply that He was the only Son of the Father God, born of a virgin, was crucified for our sins, and was resurrected three days after His burial in order to show that death had been conquered. He went ahead of us into Heaven and one day He will return. In all of that, He truly was the ONLY Son of the Father. No-one else could or can atone for the sins of mankind, nor do they need to, because Jesus' sacrifice was sufficient for all people for all time. Hallelujah!

However we can find other answers to our questions when we consider Jesus, the man. Who was He as a man? What was He like as a man? What did He do as a man? And is there any chance at all that we can be like Him?

Psychologists will tell us that every person on the face of the earth has certain basic needs, and that whether or not we succeed in life depends on whether those needs are met. Much of what we do depends on who we are, or who we perceive ourselves to be. We all need a certain sense of security and self-worth, we need to know we have an identity. To discover how God has chosen to meet these foundational needs, let us use four basic questions and relate them to Jesus' life as a man on the earth.

- Who was He?
- Where did He come from?
- Why was He born?
- Where was He going?

Who was He?

John 10.30 I and the Father are one.

Jesus describes Himself as in total unity with Father God, and He was totally confident in that role. His prayers to His Father as written in the gospels show us that he never had an identity problem. He described Himself as "at one with the Father" *(John 17:22)* The aim of the last days Sons of God is to be "at one with the Father" in the same way. To us this may seem impossible, but as that is what Jesus prayed for us it must be possible.

John 17:22 I have given them the glory that You gave Me, that they may be one as We are one.

A study of John 17 will show that this is Jesus' final prayer, and the longest one recorded in the Bible. It is a testimony to His relationship with the Father, and of how sure He was of His identity. It also answers our next question.

Where did Jesus come from?

Revelation 22:31 I am the Alpha and the Omega, the first and the last, the beginning and the end.

In heavenly terms, Jesus was never born, He always existed. He was there with the Father creator at the beginning of time, and He will be there at the end, but in earthly terms it was a very different story.

He was conceived before His mother was married and was a refugee in Egypt as a young child. The early years of Mary and Joseph's life together must not have been easy, but finally they made their home in Nazareth and became a normal working family.

We have very little information about the childhood years of Jesus, but He is mentioned as a youth when He visited Jerusalem and His parents lost Him. When they found Him in the temple, He was astounding the teachers with His knowledge. He had an understanding way beyond His years or His station in life.

Luke 2:46-47 After three days they found Him in the temple courts, sitting among the teachers, listening to them and asking them questions. Everyone who heard Him was amazed at his understanding and His answers.

The next verse tells us that His parents did not understand the situation at all, but what do we learn about Jesus from this event? In those days, for a young person to even talk to the teachers of the law in the temple they would have to be either very confident, or very audacious. Jesus certainly was very knowledgeable, and very comfortable discussing controversial religious issues with the leaders and teachers of the temple. He was not at all worried about having been separated from His family, and seemed ready to start His ministry then and there, but He returned home with his parents and waited for His Heavenly Father's perfect timing.

The fact is that Jesus was secure in who He was. He was secure in His origins. Jesus knew that He came from God even though the people around Him saw only His ordinary family. He knew even as a totally human person that God, Yahweh, was the one who had designed His birth at a certain moment in the history of the world. He knew without any shadow of a doubt that the place and moment of His birth had been prophesied in the scriptures, and had been chosen by His Heavenly Father since the beginning of creation.

Can we as human beings be so confident? I believe that we can, but that first we need to be born again into the spiritual kingdom of Heaven *(John 3:5)*. Once we are sure of our Heavenly Father, then many other things become clear.

> John 1:12-13 *Yet to all who received Him, to those who believed in His name, He gave the right to become children of God - children born not of natural descent, nor of human decision or a husband's will, but born of God.*

As we are born again into God's family through faith in Jesus, we have rights, we can claim an inheritance from Him. As we get to know God the Father on a very personal level, and by that I mean with an intimacy of love, we become more and more sure of who we are in an earthly sense.

God designed Jesus' physical birth with a specific genealogy, He chose His place of birth, and gave purpose to everything about His life, His purpose. He has done the same for you and for me. God wanted you to have the genes from the parents He chose for you. You were not a surprise to Him. He knew you before you were born, He planned your life from the beginning in order to fulfill His purposes for the earth. Maybe you are wondering what went wrong, maybe you don't feel that your parents were a blessing, perhaps you think that you come from the wrong place, were educated in the wrong way, or maybe were not educated at all. Be encouraged, God has a plan.

<u>Jeremiah 29:11</u> For I know the plans I have for you," declares the LORD, "plans to prosper you and not to harm you, plans to give you hope and a future.

Jesus was secure in the fact that He was a child of God. He talks constantly in the gospels about His Father because He knew that was where His identity lay. As Sons of God we need to have the same assurance. Although many people have learned to use the tools God gives His children, some have failed in ministry because they have never actually taken time to understand the personal relationship their Heavenly Father wants to have with them. In the twenty-one chapters of John's gospel Jesus refers thirty times to "My Father". He constantly brings our focus to this Father/Son relationship. Once we are born again and invite Jesus into our lives we become "sons of God", but creation is waiting for "Sons of God" who recognise and live in that same intimate relationship as Jesus had.

* * *

<u>Why was Jesus born?</u>

<u>John 10:10</u> I am come that you may have life, life to the full.

Many people are uncertain of the reason they were born. Many are searching for the meaning of life, and the devil is always ready to distract us from God's purposes. He did that to Jesus, and He'll do it to you. Satan knew why Jesus had come to earth, and in the temptations in the wilderness we read of the way the enemy tried to thwart the purposes of God.

> Luke 4:3-4 *The devil said to Him, "If you are the Son of God, tell this stone to become bread." Jesus answered, "It is written: 'Man does not live on bread alone'."*

First the devil questioned Jesus' identity (notice that little word "if"), but had no success with this Son of God. Jesus completely ignored the devil's subtle suggestion that things may be otherwise. How often the enemy comes at us with that little word "if". The answer is to NOT respond. We do not need to defend our identity to him, he is nothing, and we can and must be sure of ourselves as children of Father God.

The devil knew Jesus had come to do miracles and was tempting Him to do one for Himself, but Jesus replied by quoting scripture. Other than ignoring him, that is the only way to answer the enemy. Jesus did no miracle for Himself. He obeyed His heavenly Father, that was the only way He was going to pass the wilderness test.

> Luke 4:5-8 *The devil led Him up to a high place and showed Him in an instant all the kingdoms of the world. And he said to Him, "I will give you all their authority and splendour, for it has been given to me, and I can give it to anyone I want to. So if you worship me, it will all be yours." Jesus answered, "It is written: 'Worship the Lord your God and serve Him only.'"*

Satan knew that one of the callings of Jesus was to eventually rule the whole world, and he was offering a short cut. Jesus successfully avoided the trap by again speaking God's word. It is interesting that Jesus didn't resist the devil's leading Him to the high place, and He didn't deny that the authority on earth had been given to Satan, He simply quoted scripture. We must remember to not argue with the devil, or his demons, they do not have any authority over us unless we give it to them. We must know and quote scripture as Jesus did. His authority was in the Word of His Father God. Psalm 119, the longest psalm in the Bible is one which emphasizes the importance of the word of God. Jesus used the scriptures and so must we.

> Psalm 119:11 *I have hidden Your word in my heart that I might not sin against You.*

Ask yourself how much of God's word is hidden in your heart? Do you know enough of the Bible to quote it under pressure?

As we read the gospels we find several reasons that Jesus Himself gave us for His coming to earth, one of the best reasons is quoted above, and repeated here.

> John 10:10 *...I have come that they may have life, and have it to the full.*

If we understand that full, abundant life which is promised by Jesus, then we can share it with others. We can go to the hurting, the sick, the abused, and we can tell them that Jesus came to give them life to the full today. We can go in His name, using His authority. Near the end of John's gospel, we read the reason for John's writing his version of Jesus' earthly life :

> John 20:31 *But these are written that you may believe that Jesus is the Christ, the Son of God, and that by believing you may have life in His name.*

Jesus' purpose (to tell others of the life God has for them) had become John's purpose. Is it yours? Is it mine?

Jesus' awareness of who He was, and why He had come to earth can be found throughout the gospels. He was never intimidated by the opposition, although He did get angry with them from time to time. We must become secure enough in Him to not be phased by the opposition which will surely come our way as we go out in His name. Jesus warned His disciples that there would be lots of enemy activity, lots of aggression, abuse and attacks, but He also told them not to be bothered by it, or let it stop them. Rather, He told them to rejoice in the truth of who He was and who they were in Him. *(Matthew 5:11 & Luke 21:11 & John 15:20)*

* * *

Where was He going?

Jesus knew His future and He knew His destiny. He was fully aware that once His ministry started He had only a very short time until it would be over. He knew what an incredibly painful end it would be to His physical life here on the earth, and yet He continued to follow God's plan. He went all the way out of love for us. He talked of His cross, long before any one else understood that that was where he was heading, and He told others to take up their cross too.

> Matthew 16:24 & Luke 9:23 *"If anyone would come after Me, he must deny himself and take up his cross and follow Me."*

Please note that we are not to carry Jesus' cross for Him, He did that Himself. Each of us is to carry our own cross. The cross was Jesus' destiny. Taking up your personal cross means to enter into your destiny as designed by God. It means only doing what the Father is showing you to do, only saying what the Father gives you to say, it means obedience in every area of life. That is the sort of Son of God that creation is waiting for.

Jesus knew the difficulties and the suffering that were ahead of Him, but He also knew the glories of Heaven that came after that. He had already experienced life in Heaven at His Father's side. We can only imagine what that is like. He knew what it meant for His Spirit to be free to fly with the angels, something that most of us can hardly even imagine. Jesus knew the rewards of His obedience, and the Bible gives us indications of what is ahead for us too.

The book of Revelation gives us wonderful pictures of Heaven and the new existence that we will have after Jesus comes back to reign on the earth.

> Revelation 21:4 *He will wipe every tear from their eyes. There will be no more death or mourning or crying or pain, for the old order of things has passed away.*

John records for us in the book of Revelation the visions he had of God's future Kingdom once all evil is destroyed. Others too have had visions of the Heavenly kingdom. More and more Christians are receiving revelation about the next life and our rewards in Heaven. Creation is waiting for the Real Sons of God who will get a grip of the vision and the calling; the vision of life with the Lord today as well as in the future, and the calling of God's purpose for their own personal life. Stepping into the reality of that vision and calling and running with it is what it means to take up your cross.

* * *

Many books have been written to encourage us to do what Jesus did, and most of us have heard messages taught on the final instructions of Jesus, left to us at the end of Matthew's gospel. The eleven disciples had all met the risen Jesus, they had been rebuked for their lack of faith, and I can imagine that they were thoroughly confused. They never knew if or when Jesus was going to appear again. He seemed able to come through locked doors, as though He were a ghost, but then He ate breakfast with them after He had prepared a barbecue on the beach. *(John 21:12-13)* This was not at all like a ghost. They believed He was meant to be the King of the Jews, but how could they plan any sort of campaign if He kept appearing and disappearing?

Then one day He told them to meet Him on top of a mountain. Can you imagine their enthusiasm as they climbed up there hoping for a planning meeting for the next stage in the Kingdom they were sure He was ready to establish? But instead of starting a campaign to claim a throne, Jesus gave them a farewell speech.

> <u>Matthew 28:18-20</u> *Then Jesus came to them and said, "All authority in heaven and on earth has been given to Me. Therefore go and make disciples of all nations, baptising them in the name of the Father and of the Son and of the Holy Spirit, and teaching them to obey everything I have commanded you. And surely I am with you always, to the very end of the age."*

This was not exactly how they had planned it. Luke tells us in Acts chapter one that they were still asking questions about the coming kingdom.

> <u>Acts 1:6</u> *So when they met together, they asked him, "Lord, are You at this time going to restore the kingdom to Israel?"*

They had not understood at all. What Jesus was saying was, in effect, "I've done all I am going to do, now it's up to you. You go. You perform the miracles. You tell people about me. Yes, I will be a King in the Kingdom, but not just for Israel, for the whole world. Now I'm waiting for you to do the rest!" But then He told them not to do anything until they had been empowered from on high, and we know that happened on the day of Pentecost when the Holy Spirit radically changed each one of them, and the first church gained 3000 members in one day.

> *Matthew 28:18-20 Then Jesus came to them and said, "All authority in heaven and on earth has been given to me. Therefore go and make disciples of all nations, baptising them in the name of the Father and of the Son and of the Holy Spirit,and teaching them to obey everything I have commanded you. And surely I am with you always, to the very end of the age."*

Not only have books been written and sermons preached on the last words of Jesus, known as the great commission, but churches have begun because of it. Many missionary organisations have been started because of that phrase beginning "*Therefore go*". The same words have inspired the whole Evangelical movement, and it seems obvious that the next part of the verse, *"baptising them in the name of the Father and of the Son and of the Holy Spirit"* had some influence in the birth of Baptist churches all across the world. Different people have been inspired by different verses or parts of verses and have had different reactions, with the result today that we have many different denominations. How boring it would be if all churches were identical and with the same emphasis!

But, whatever happened to the first phrase of His instructions? Jesus declared: *"All authority in heaven and on earth has been given to me."* So many people have gone out into the world not understanding His authority. If we knew how much authority we really have as believers, then the 'going' and the 'making disciples' would both be much easier than many people find them. The end of John's gospel puts it a different way.

> *John 20:21* *Again Jesus said, "Peace be with you! As the Father has sent Me, I am sending you."*

In the same way that Father God sent Jesus out on His life's mission, so Jesus sends us out on our life's mission. Please note that Jesus no longer talks of "My Father" as He has done so often in the gospel account, but "The Father", meaning the Father of all, and signifying that He is the Father of those who follow Him.

If Jesus sends us out in the same way that He was sent, it means as a Son of God.

That means with the same authority. Creation is waiting for those sons who understand Father God, have a close relationship with Him as Jesus did, and who move in His authority. It is as though Jesus is saying to us today "Go, knowing that I am with you, that I am all you need. Creation is waiting for you."

Chapter 11

Becoming Like Little Children

Matthew 18:3 And He said: "I tell you the truth, unless you change and become like little children, you will never enter the kingdom of heaven.

I have been thinking a lot about this verse and what it actually means. In the past, I have heard sermons on the innocence of children and how we need to get rid of our sins and become pure and childlike. But I'm not so sure that is the right way to look at this Gospel passage.

As I have observed children in different environments in different nations and in different cultural situations, I have come to believe that innocence is not the primary thought when you watch a group of siblings playing together.

Children left to themselves are :

- Not nice at all.
- Messy and dirty.
- Totally self centred.
- Cruel to each other.
- Liars if the occasion demands.
- Argumentative.

- Greedy.
- They push against any boundaries, real or imagined.
- They get into places they shouldn't.
- They help themselves to what they want, secretly if they have to. (Is this stealing?)
- They are undisciplined and uncontrolled.
- They fight.
- They are very easily influenced in the wrong direction.

Maybe you think I am being too hard, but as a grandmother of eleven I can assure you that each one of my eleven grandchildren has had to be trained. I love them all dearly of course, but I know that without their parental discipline life would have been very hard for them, and they would be growing into selfish adults or even vandals. Even after quite a lot of parental teaching, at least until their early teens, each one has still been ready to fight for the biggest piece of cake, ready to shout if they think that another has more than is fair.

Without the discipline of their parents every one of them would have terrible table manners, would rarely wash themselves or clean their teeth. They would hardly ever do their homework, and would happily get their siblings into trouble if they thought they could get away with something themselves. For every lesson they have learned, there has had to be repeated teachings as well as repeated punishments for wrong actions, and of course many repeated encouragements when things have been done the right way.

Without those things most of the children I know would have run across the road without looking, have gone off with a stranger, or eaten poisonous fruit in the forest. Discipline is necessary and good, and I am convinced that without it no child would make very much of life. If you thought Jesus was thinking "innocence and purity" when He talked about children, think again.

So what did the perfect Son of the perfect Father mean when He took a child and talked about becoming like one of them. Which of the characteristics in the list quoted above was He thinking of?

Perhaps the last quality on the list is the one to start with! If children can be easily influenced in the wrong direction, then maybe they are easily influenced in the right direction too. I am not convinced we can put the word "easily" in there. Most parents will say that children are naturally selfish and have to be trained to think of others and to do the right things the right way. Not necessarily an easy task.

Of course what is right and what is wrong depends on the culture a family lives in, it depends on traditions and trends, race and creed, but in every case it is true that a child has to be trained in all those things. A child needs to be educated.

It is important to note that the verse above talks of "little children", and in the Mark version of this story, Jesus took the little child in his arms, so we suppose that

He is talking about a toddler, aged around two or three years. A child who is still learning everything. One who is not already too far into bad habits that he cannot be taught a different way.

Let's write a list of good qualities of a small child to balance the depressing list above.

Most small children are:

- Teachable.
- Eager to learn.
- Eager to please.
- Trusting.
- Faithful in friendships.
- Quick to forgive and be friends again after an argument.
- Ready to forget their disappointments.
- Ready to copy an adult.
- Quick to believe the supernatural.

Jesus said "unless you change". Those listening to Him needed to change! Jesus was talking to his disciples, not the regular crowd who followed Him wanting to be healed and to see miracles. We can suppose there was a crowd round about because someone close by had a child, but it was the query of the disciples that prompted the lesson. Jesus was answering their question about who is the greatest in the Kingdom, and He replied by referring to the humility of a child. Let's look at the verse in context.

> *Matthew 18:1-6 At that time the disciples came to Jesus and asked, "Who is the greatest in the kingdom of*

Heaven?" He called a little child and had him stand among them. And he said: "I tell you the truth, unless you change and become like little children, you will never enter the kingdom of heaven. Therefore, whoever humbles himself like this child is the greatest in the kingdom of heaven. And whoever welcomes a little child like this in My name welcomes Me. But if anyone causes one of these little ones who believe in Me to sin, it would be better for him to have a large millstone hung around his neck and to be drowned in the depths of the sea.

Do you see how the child humbled himself? Jesus called him and he came. He was willing to stand in front of the group and be used as a visual aid. Most adults are not so ready to do that. But the child recognised that he could trust Jesus. He knew instinctively that this man was not going to make fun of him or have everyone laugh at him. Do you know that you can trust Jesus one hundred per cent of the time. Are you ready to be used by Him and for Him as a visual aid?

If we, the followers of Jesus are to change and become like little children, what do we need to do? I am fairly certain that the Lord does not want us to have all the disagreeable child-like qualities listed at the beginning of this chapter, but He does want us to take on the characteristics of the second list.

The Greek word used in our Bible verse for change is "*strepho*" and it means to convert or to do an about-turn. It is not talking about a gradual change, but a decision to go in another direction. We have to stop thinking in the way we have thought for much of our lives, we have to do an about-turn in our thinking and our attitudes. Jesus wants us to "be converted" in more ways than one. Let's look again at the list of good childlike qualities, and as we do that, ask yourself how much you need to be converted.

Children are teachable

The more I learn about the Lord, the more I find there is to know. How sad it is that so many people are converted to Christianity and think that is the end. They have their ticket to Heaven, and nothing more is to be done. How wrong they are, we must remain teachable.

The Lord has so much more for us than we have so far experienced, no matter how long we have been believers. Real Sons of God are prepared at every moment for their Heavenly Father to teach them something new. It may be something about the future, something about what He did in the past, or just something fun to learn because he is a fun Father to learn from.

One of the problems I see in many adults is the inability to be taught by others. Pride gets in the way. Everyone of those people would say they are ready to learn from the Lord, but few of them recognize that He uses others to teach us. He uses difficulties, He uses children, He uses other people, and unfortunately those are often the people we find difficult to get along with, not always those who are more mature in the faith. The Father who loves us has a multitude of ways of teaching us, and we must be ready to learn the maximum from every situation, and from every person He brings across our paths.

Children are eager to Learn

Once a son of God understands the constant presence of Holy Spirit in his life, he should be eager to learn in every situation. The more I get to know the Bible, the more I want to study it in depth, to get behind the translation I am reading and try to understand the Greek and Hebrew of the original text. Yes it has so much to say to us in our preferred version, whether in modern or more traditional text, but comparing verses in different versions brings an abundance of depth to the meaning, and reading something in the language it was written in brings even more revelation. Holy Spirit is more than ready to teach. If we are not constantly learning something new it is our fault, not His.

The learning process must be expanded to everything we experience, not just the spiritual lessons we are trying to learn from our daily Bible readings. If we are looking for them, we will see the confirmations of these lessons in the small things that happen to us seemingly by chance. Nothing is by chance and every "coincidence" is really a "God-incidence". Look for them and keep learning.

Children are eager to Please

Children are eager to please those in charge, whether teachers, carers or parents. It is part of the need to be accepted and loved. Very quickly a child will learn what is acceptable behaviour in different situations, in the classroom, at home or at grandma's house. They will generally adapt their behaviour accordingly in order to please the older person.

Sons of God know how to please their Father God and are conscious that it is a totally different thing than trying to please a person, especially someone in authority. To become those who are eager to please the Lord, we have to understand that it is not the same as being a man-pleaser. We need to remember that God sees our intentions, and not our outward behaviour. Hebrews 4:12 tells us that His word judges the thoughts and attitudes of the heart. He knows who we are trying to please.

Sons of God are those who have learned to be God-pleasers instead of man-pleasers, and are eager to please Him twenty-four hours a day. The best way to please our Heavenly Father is just to spend time in His presence, to develop that Father/son relationship. Everything else comes from there.

Children are trusting

In a normal well-functioning family, a small child trusts his parents implicitly. No questions asked. There is total confidence that everything the child needs and that is good for him will be provided at the right time.

Have you ever seen a child tossing and turning at night because they couldn't pay a bill or didn't know what to eat for lunch the following day? Does a child worry about what to wear? There is total confidence that the person responsible is ready to provide those things at the right moment. Trusting our Heavenly Father needs to be the same. Can we really put our lives in His hands in the same way that a small child trusts a loving parent or guardian?

Children are faithful in friendships

Small children will quickly learn which other children they like and which they don't, and once friendships are made they are generally long lasting. Friends will help each other, play together, learn together, experiment life together, and be naughty together if the situation allows. Most adults can remember the good times as well as the mischievous times with certain childhood friendships.

Christianity was never meant to be a lonely path. When you become a son of God you join a huge family and will find brothers, sisters and friends who will be faithful no matter what. Sons of God are those who help, encourage, and learn with others. What we learn is meant to be shared with the rest of the family so that all can benefit.

Children are quick to forgive and be friends again after an argument

Children are quick to fight, and quick to forgive. Most children are ready to throw a brick at their best friend if something goes wrong, and many a parent has had to intervene to stop children scratching, hair-pulling, biting, or kicking each other. The important thing for our lesson here is that kids don't bear grudges. Once the fight is over, it is over.

How many church splits would have been avoided if the warring parties had been able to be childlike and forgive and forget? None of us in the body of Christ has all the answers. The things on which churches disagree were never meant to be dividing issues forever, but they were meant to be complimentary. The church was meant to function as a body, each part doing what it is called to do and what it does best. No arguments!

Children are ready to forget their disappointments

When a child asks a parent for something and the request is not granted, there will be disappointment, but it will not last long. And it will certainly not deter the child from asking again for the same thing on a different occasion. Too many of us have been disappointed by friends, by family, and by the church, and many of us feel disappointed with God. The result can be that we have distanced ourselves from the source of the disappointment.

If you feel you have been let down by others, especially those in the church, you may have withdrawn from that community. If, as an adult you have asked the Lord for something that you have not yet received, you may well have kept that disappointment in your heart. The result is that you don't think you can trust that person or the Lord again. Deep inside, the next time you want to pray for something or somebody you remember the unanswered prayers, the times when you felt let down, and you can't ask with confidence or in faith.

Children do not have that problem, neither do they have to go through deliverance before they can ask for anything else. As mature adults, we need to learn from the child who is quick to let go of disappointments, the child who doesn't bear a grudge.

Tell the Lord today that you forgive Him for those times in the past both distant or recent, when you felt He let you down. Acknowledge that His ways are not your ways, and let go of those "stones" that are heavy in your heart. Make a decision today to forgive those people who have let you down in the past. They are only human like you, they too are learning to be childlike.

Children are ready to copy an adult

Small children learn by copying. Obviously those who have good role models fare better than those who don't. For adults who are trying to change and become childlike, what better role model is there than Jesus? He was the perfect copier. He only ever did what He saw the Father doing *(John 5:19)*. If we copy Him then we cannot go wrong.

It is important to note that I am not necessarily talking about what the church does, but what Jesus does or did. Sadly so much of the church does not do what Jesus did at all. He never did what the Pharisees expected Him to do, and He caused quite a few disturbances as a result. But by copying what His Father did, He succeeded in healing the sick, casting out demons and raising the dead. Are you ready to copy Him?

Children are not afraid

A normal child does not see too many dangers, but has to be taught about them by an adult. Of course it is essential that we teach our children not to step onto the road in the way of the traffic. It is essential that we teach them not to drink poisonous substances, but what about climbing mountains? What about racing downhill on a bike? What about swinging high? A wise and caring adult must be able to teach about danger without limiting a child. We, like them, should not be limited by our fears.

Does fear stop you from going higher with the Lord?

Does fear stop you from going further with the Lord?

Does fear make you put limits that are too tight on your children?

Ask the Lord to help you overcome your fears today.

Children are quick to believe the supernatural

Small children believe in fairies, dragons, angels, talking trees and talking animals as well as all sorts of other make-believe creatures because of the films they see, the books they look at, or the stories that adults read to them. It is only because of the things they are taught later that these things cease to exist in their minds.

The way we are educated has a lot to do with who we are today as adults, and as sons of God. Too many of us need to get back to a "childlike faith", or maybe even to a childish faith. One that simply believes that what God says is true and that He **will** do **everything** He promises when the time is right.

Our educated adult minds know that what God says is true and that He can do whatever He wants. There is a huge difference here between the two auxiliary verbs "will" and "can". A childlike faith, and a childlike belief in the supernatural changes the "can" to "will"! Do you believe that what God says is true and that He **will** do everything He says?

If you tell a child that Jesus lives in his heart and that Jesus wants to heal people, the child will believe you. Then if you suggest that the child goes to tell somebody else this truth and pray for them, most of them will do it.

What is stopping us becoming like little children? Let's get rid of the hindrances of adult thinking and "just do it".

Chapter 12

Parents Of The End-Time Sons

Many of the people reading this book will be over the age of thirty, and many of you will be quite a long way past that age. You will be the mothers and fathers, and in many cases grandparents, of the last generation being prepared by the Lord to be His end-time children. You may be one who has no children, but has been chosen to be a godparent or to mentor some of this generation. What a privilege each one of us has, and what a responsibility! You will be the people who have interceded for years for the generation prepared to usher in the millennium. You are the spiritual parents of many who have been called for such a time as this. Is there anything you can still do, now that the Lord is answering your prayers and raising up His Sons?

As I travel and speak this message out across the nations, my cry to the sons of God is: "Just do it! Dare to become Real Sons of God that creation is waiting for." Just allow yourself to do what God is calling you to do, no matter how crazy, how futile, how strange it may seem to you and those around you. Jesus did EVERYTHING His father asked Him to do, and it worked the other way too. Father God did everything the Son asked Him to do. That's the sort of relationship the end-time sons will have with their Heavenly Father.

But I cry out to the parents too, and my plea is "Let them go!" Step back from the roles you have played until now. You were God's instrument to birth this child, or maybe to adopt him or her. You were chosen to educate them and cooperate with the Lord up to a certain point, but there comes a time for the Holy Spirit to take over much more of that parenting role.

Parents need to let their children go and grow. Obviously the amount of letting go will vary according to the age of the child, but there is much that applies to any age. We, as parents, must let Father God parent our children. He will do a much better job than we ourselves could ever do. To hand our offspring over to the Lord is not just a sitting back and opting out, it is a very positive thing. It means that we study the scriptures and see what they say about raising the next generation. It means taking seriously verses like those in Proverbs, in spite of modern trends in child care.

> Proverbs 19:18 *Discipline your son, for in that there is hope; do not be a willing party to his death.*

> Proverbs 23:13 *Do not withhold discipline from a child; if you punish him with the rod, he will not die.*

Proverbs 23:14 Punish him with the rod and save his soul from death.

Please note that I am not advocating beating a child. Modern trends in child care mean that many parents are saying "we don't spank them, we reason with them". Or the attitude is: "He is only a baby, he doesn't know yet that this (or that) is wrong." My response to that attitude is: your child will never get it right if he is not shown repeatedly **not** to do certain things! As those responsible for bringing up well-behaved, obedient children, we must realise that they are not naturally good, they are naturally selfish, and need to be taught what is right and wrong. A baby needs to learn what is good and what is bad, but most of all he needs to know that "no" means "no"! God doesn't debate with us the right and wrongs of His rules, when He says no, He means no, not "maybe", or "later if I am in a good mood".

Consistency is one of the most important things in disciplining our children. If we allow a certain behaviour or attitude one day, and don't the next day just because of our own mood changes, or because we are busier, then we are not being helpful at all. Father God never has mood changes. He is totally consistent in everything. In His love for us, in what He says we must not do, and in what He says we must do. Praise Him that He never changes *(James 1:17)*.

We must teach our kids to be obedient to their parents, no matter what the request. The earlier they learn this, the easier life will be for all concerned. Learning obedience to our earthly fathers is the best practice-run for learning obedience to God. If a child has been allowed to argue with his earthly father and only obey when he feels like it, he will not obey Father God, and our future Sons of God could well find themselves in life and death situations where hearing and obeying God is of the utmost importance.

Hebrews chapter 12 has a lot to say about the Lord's discipline, comparing it to that of earthly fathers.

> Hebrews 12:7-11 *Endure hardship as discipline; God is treating you as sons. For what son is not disciplined by his father? If you are not disciplined (and everyone undergoes discipline), then you are illegitimate children and not true sons. Moreover, we have all had human fathers who disciplined us and we respected them for it. How much more should we submit to the Father of our spirits and live! Our fathers disciplined us for a little while as they thought best; but God disciplines us for our good, that we may share in His holiness. No discipline seems pleasant at the time, but painful. Later on, however, it produces a harvest of righteousness and peace for those who have been trained by it.*

Sadly, family breakdowns mean that many people alive today did not have fathers who disciplined them.

Even those children with both parents at home can suffer from a lack of good parenting. Fathers and mothers who are not strict with their offspring are doing them no favours. Children need to have limits, and the limits need to be well established while the children are small. Boundaries can be enlarged as children grow, but it is far easier to extend them from limited beginnings than it is to draw them in after a bad start with no rules.

It does not take a psychologist to tell us that lots of repairing needs to be done in so many lives today! The world is full of "un-parented" children The church community needs to be prepared to parent those who have not had "normal" family life. Most important, the church family needs to do that in love, wisdom and without any judging or condemnation.

Being responsible in any way for this generation means praying and praying and praying again for ourselves as parents, grandparents, godparents and mentors as well as for our children as they grow in knowledge of the Lord. Let us train our children to listen to the Lord and to obey, so that they may "share in His holiness", and reap that "harvest of righteousness and peace" *(Hebrews 12:10-11).*

* * *

As I looked into the need for a parental "letting go", I became more and more convinced of my own personal need to repent of much in regard to my own children. I became aware of how much my husband and I have brought our children up to be like us, their physical parents. We have taught them to do things our way, which is not wrong; we are law-abiding citizens, we are loving parents who have given much to our children, the best we knew how to give at the time. But we did not teach them to do things God's way. We taught them to think in the same way we do, convinced of course that we were right, totally logical and reasonable. But I am now reminded of one of my favourite Old Testament verses:

> Isaiah 55:8-9 *"For My thoughts are not your thoughts, neither are your ways My ways," declares the LORD. "As the heavens are higher than the earth, so are My ways higher than your ways and My thoughts than your thoughts."*

I cannot count how many times I have quoted that verse, usually when I don't understand what God is doing, then I use it as a let-out clause saying: "Oh well, God's ways aren't my ways". However, when I look at how we have brought up our children in the light of this new understanding of Father God, then I recognize that we were aiming for much less than God wanted for them and for us.

I remember one time when I was quoting that verse back to God because I couldn't comprehend what He was trying to tell me, and I was hoping He would explain things further, when suddenly I felt like he was telling me to find the verse in the Bible and read it properly, so I did. I read it out to Him several times and told Him that I agreed with every word. He is so far above me in intelligence, in wisdom, in understanding, that I can't hope to grasp even the smallest part of it. He listened patiently to my futile words, then He told me to read the rest of the passage. (Remember when I said in the first chapter that there can be a danger in taking Bible verses out of context.) Of course it is a wonderful chapter with much to teach us, but the verse that I finally got a hold of that day was the one which precedes the two quoted above which are so well known.

> Isaiah 55:7-9 *Let the wicked forsake his way and the evil man his thoughts. Let him turn to the LORD, and He will have mercy on him, and to our God, for He will freely pardon. "For My thoughts are not your thoughts, neither are your ways My ways," declares the LORD. "As the heavens are higher than the earth, so are My ways higher than your ways and My thoughts than your thoughts."*

Suddenly, reading that first sentence, I knew as I had never known before that every thought I have which was not totally in line with those of the Lord put me in the category of "evil". I was shocked, and began to understand afresh why St. Paul insists on the renewing of our minds *(Romans 12:2)*. As parents, most of us, probably all of us, have had thoughts, opinions and ideas about our children that are not in line with God's thoughts.

Yes, the majority of us have done our best, but not one of us has been a perfect parent, because only God can be the perfect parent. It is not our fault that we have fallen short of perfection, because none of us had perfect parents either, and so we have brought up our own children out of our own experiences, out of our own ideas, our own hopes and ambitions, and we have consequently burdened our kids with those things that were not theirs to carry or to experience. The Lord has given me a quick painless prayer of repentance which can change a lot, and I include it here:

> *Father God, I am beginning to realize my failings as a parent. I have always known that You were the only perfect parent, but too often I have left You out of the equation. Too often I have done what I thought best for my kids without consulting You at all. You know Lord that most of this happened before I knew You as I now know You, and I thank You that You have been there through all my mistakes, and I thank You that You have prevented me from making many more than I actually made.*
>
> *Father I want to say I am sorry for raising my children to be like me, and not like You. I want to say I am sorry for allowing myself to be the role model when it should have been You. I recognize that my aim was to have children I could be proud of, without thinking whether or not the same actions would make You proud of them. I recognize that I wanted offspring who would hold high my family name, when all the time it should have been Your name they were carrying.*

Father, forgive me for not allowing You to be more involved in the parenting of my children, forgive me for trying to take Your place. Lord I repent of my foolishness, and I ask You to take my children, and let them be truly Yours. Correct the things that need correcting, adjust things where adjustments are necessary, bless them Lord with Your inheritance and let them be Real Sons of God that You can be proud of, in Jesus name. Amen.

In Matthew chapter 10, a passage I have often referred to as the Jesus Bible School, Jesus prepares His disciples for going out on their first missionary trip. He starts by equipping them to cast out demons and heal the sick, but then things become more complicated. It's as though He first gives the good news, then later in the chapter He gives the bad news, and the bad news gets worse and worse until we reach verse thirty-four:

> *Matthew 10:34-36 Do not suppose that I have come to bring peace to the earth. I did not come to bring peace, but a sword. For I have come to turn "'a man against his father, a daughter against her mother, a daughter-in-law against her mother-in-law - a man's enemies will be the members of his own household.'*

The way we have educated our children, the way we have taught them to think can be a trap of the enemy for them, because Isaiah says that our ways are not His ways. The sword which Jesus brought, and speaks about here is the word of God which speaks so much louder than anything parents have ever said to their children. If we cannot repent and release our children in this time to go out and obey the Lord, then they will have no choice but to take that sword of the spirit and be cut off from us.

The choice is ours to try to hang onto them, and consequently lose them, or to let them go with a blessing and prayer for them to move into all that the Lord has for them. The demands of the Lord on their lives in these coming years will be so strong that if we do not bless them and let them go, we will lose them entirely. Which of us in our hearts wants to say to our children;- "Don't do what God is telling you, stay here and do what I say"? I'm sure very few of us want that, but if we don't free our kids to be the Sons the Lord is calling forth, then that is what we will be doing. We will become the enemies in the household quoted above.

When St. Paul was taken before King Agrippa, he told the story of his miraculous conversion, and in this account, he gives some details that we don't read in the first account in Acts chapter 9. It is the Lord speaking to Paul:

> Acts 26:16-17 *Now get up and stand on your feet. I have appeared to you to appoint you as a servant and as a witness of what you have seen of Me and what I will show you. I will rescue you from your own people and from the Gentiles.*

When I read that word "rescue", I asked myself "why would Saul need rescuing from his own people?" Of course the Jews were to become some of St. Paul's strongest critics, they were to stone him, whip him, imprison him, and he would need rescuing on many occasions. But the Lord used this word before any of that happened, because it has a wider meaning than being rescued from harm. I believe that Saul needed to be "rescued" from his family line, from his heritage, from the expectations of his parents, even though they are never mentioned. He was going to have to denounce everything they had hoped for him, everything he himself had worked and studied hard to possess.

The word "rescue" is not used in every Bible translation, but in the Greek the word is "*exairew*", which means to deliver, to rescue, to pluck out, to release. Whichever way you read it, Saul had to be separated from his own people. When the Lord met with him on the Damascus road, He plucked him out of one life style and launched him into something totally different. God wants to do the same with many of our children, and we must let them go. All of our children need to be "rescued" from their families, even good families. They need to become Real Sons of God (RSGs), true believers, the ones creation is waiting for.

Those who are true believers will do what the Bible says they will do. If you are a parent of a last-days Son of

God, you should be encouraging your child to live up to the Biblical standard of a believer. Let's just look at a few appropriate verses before closing this chapter, and let's allow these verses to challenge us.

> Matthew 21:22 ***If you believe***, *you will receive whatever you ask for in prayer. (Emphasis mine)*

Do we teach our children that they can have "whatever they ask for", or do we tell them that God doesn't always answer our prayers and make excuses for Him just in case He doesn't answer their present prayer? How can we encourage them to believe for **everything** they ask for, and to ask only for what they hear the Father saying?

> Mark 16:17-18 *And these signs will accompany those who believe: In my name they will drive out demons; they will speak in new tongues; they will pick up snakes with their hands; and when they drink deadly poison, it will not hurt them at all; they will place their hands on sick people, and they will get well."*

Parents, please note the confidence in this verse. It does not say these signs **might** accompany, but these signs will (definitely) accompany those who believe.

> Mark 9:23 *"Everything is possible for him who believes."*

How big a word is "everything" for you? For me? For our children?

> Mark 11:23 *"I tell you the truth, if anyone says to this mountain, 'Go, throw yourself into the sea,' and does*

not doubt in his heart but believes that what he says will happen, it will be done for him.

Believing, speaking and receiving should be the principals we are teaching our children, all encompassed in love, of course. If we have not taught our children the love of Father God, then we have taught them nothing. If they do not understand being a well-beloved child of the perfect Father, then they can do as much speaking to mountains and believing in their collapse as they like, it will not happen. God's first priority for this last generation, as it has been for every other generation, is to have children who love Him and understand His love for them. Everything comes out of that.

John 6:35 Then Jesus declared, "I am the bread of life. He who comes to Me will never go hungry, and he who believes in Me will never be thirsty.

This verse has two meanings, one physical and one spiritual. Jesus wants to satisfy every need, both physical, emotional and spiritual. Do we believe He can do that? Do we believe He will?

John 1:12 Yet to all who received Him, to those who believed in His name, He gave the right to become children of God.

Rights have to be claimed. Parents need to be teaching their children that they have the right to step out of the earthly parental inheritance and into their Heavenly one. The family tree that comes down from God the Father has no sickness, no debts, no family quirks, no curses. Just good things! Hallelujah!

John 7:38 Whoever believes in Me, as the Scripture has said, streams of living water will flow from within him."

Jesus did not talk about a little stream, a little trickle of water. He only ever talked in abundant language. Personally, I have been very challenged by this verse, I asked myself how much living water flowed through me. I was not too encouraged by the truthful response the Lord had me give to my own question. I recognised that unless water is flowing somewhere it becomes stagnant. Are today's parents teaching their children to let the love of Jesus flow through them to others? Do we as parents allow that water to flow through us, or do we keep it for ourselves? The Lord wants to use all of us as channels for His love touching others. Let's do that, and let's encourage our children to do the same.

Being a parent is never easy, being a parent of the Real Sons of God for the last days may be even more difficult, but the Lord is constantly there to encourage and help us. What a privilege it will be to see our children so in love with Jesus that they will do anything and everything for Him. How we will rejoice when we see miracles at their hands, when we see our world being changed drastically by the next generation, by our own children, because they are God's own children. Real Sons of God. Hallelujah!

Chapter 13

Creation

No book with the word "creation" in the title would be complete without at least a brief look at what we mean by that word. When Paul wrote the verse that prompted this whole study in His letter to the Romans, what did he actually mean? We have looked a lot at who the sons of God are, but what about creation? What exactly did he mean when he said that the creation is waiting. Are the birds and the bees, the animal kingdom waiting for something? Is the dust of the earth holding it's breath until something miraculous happens in these last days? Are the trees waving their arms and calling out Hallelujah to the Lord above them? It all sounds a bit far fetched doesn't it? But I think there is a certain amount of truth in these comments and questions. Here is the verse in context:

Romans 8:19-22 *The creation waits in eager expectation for the Sons of God to be revealed. For the creation was subjected to frustration, not by its own choice, but by the will of the One who subjected it, in hope that the creation itself will be liberated from its bondage to decay and brought into the glorious freedom of the children of*

God. We know that the whole creation has been groaning as in the pains of childbirth right up to the present time.

According to the Genesis account, God created the whole universe and all that it contains before He created the first person, Adam, His first son. A little later, although we have no idea how much later, God gave Adam his partner, Eve. At that time, everything and everyone was fulfilled and blessed. There were no problems, no arguments, no illness, no sorrow. Life consisted of happiness, peace, joy, and excitement as creation revealed its secrets to Adam and Eve. Can you imagine that garden? That's what Heaven will be like. All the difficulties, pain, and curses which arrived as a result of the first sin will be non-existent once more. So many of us believers are waiting for that day when Heaven is brought to earth, when Jesus comes back to rule and reign, but we forget, or maybe we have never even thought that "creation" is waiting for that too.

Genesis 3:17 *"Cursed is the ground because of you; through painful toil you will eat of it all the days of your life.*

Creation itself was cursed, the ground of the earth received the anger of God. Eve was given pain in childbirth, but Adam himself was not actually cursed. He suffered as result of the curse put on the ground and also the one put on his wife. Creation, on the other hand, has been suffering directly ever since sin entered it, and will continue to be under that curse until those who are truly living as Sons of God fulfill their purpose. After God raises up those Sons who actually live as Jesus did, after the Real Sons of God move into their destiny, then will come the return of Jesus and the fulfillment of all things.

In the last verse in the Romans passage above, Paul says: *"We know that the whole creation has been groaning...."*. I wish I knew what Paul knew, because I cannot say that I understand these things, can you? There are lots of people who have seen and heard things in the spirit, and have confirmed what Paul is saying, but personally I have to say it is just one of those things I believe because the Bible says it. I am aware that the understanding of the science of sound is progressing rapidly and modern technology has allowed us to hear sounds we didn't know existed several years ago. I am sure it won't be long before somebody plays a recording of what nature is saying to us. Maybe we'll be surprised when we hear the groans of the earth.

As I was preparing this book I read the following comment on my computer one day, it so confirmed what I was thinking about that I would like to quote it here.

From the desk of Steve Shultz:[1]

> *Just recently, I was praying literally for the earth. Now I'm not "Mr. Eco" or a "tree hugger" but I believe it when the Word of God says that all creation is groaning, waiting in expectation for the manifestations of the sons*

[1]Steve Shultz : www.elijahlist.com

(and daughters of course) of God. As I prayed for the literal earth, I began to weep and sob and quote that Scripture from memory (Romans 8:19-25). I believe every last blade of grass is groaning for God to complete the Master Plan.

If we look back at the creation story, we can see that God created man in His own image, and He gave him (us) the responsibility to care for His creation. A study of the deeper meaning behind the Hebrew words used in Genesis 1:28 would show that man was supposed to behave as God did in bringing order over the chaos. The last-days Sons of God will finally fulfil this command. They will move into the authority and the command given to Adam.

> Genesis 1:28 *..."Be fruitful and increase in number; fill the earth and subdue it."*

Is that command really so different to the one given by Jesus to His disciples? Aren't we still supposed to be multiplying our numbers of believers, and taking authority over everything? Creation is waiting for that. It is up to you and me, the Sons of God today to redress the balance.

The scriptures tell us that Jesus came as the second Adam to change things back to how God intended them to be.

> 1 Corinthians 15:22 *For as in Adam all die, so in Christ all will be made alive.*

1 Corinthians 15:45 So it is written: "The first man Adam became a living being"; the last Adam, a life-giving spirit.

Jesus came to show us how to live; He came to give us a renewed command from the Lord, so that we could put things right and so that He could return. Jesus showed us His authority over created things in the story of the fig tree, in the changing of water into wine, and in the stilling of the storm. He gave that same authority to us, creation is waiting for us to use it.

The Fig Tree

Matthew 21:18-22 Early in the morning, as Jesus was on His way back to the city, He was hungry. Seeing a fig-tree by the road, He went up to it but found nothing on it except leaves. Then He said to it, "May you never bear fruit again!" Immediately the tree withered. When the disciples saw this, they were amazed. "How did the fig-tree wither so quickly?" they asked. Jesus replied, "I tell you the truth, if you have faith and do not doubt, not only can you do what was done to the fig-tree, but also you can say to this mountain, 'Go, throw yourself into the sea,' and it will be done. If you believe, you will receive whatever you ask for in prayer."

Jesus expected to find figs on the tree because the reason for its existence was to produce figs. Nature was designed to serve mankind; it was meant to provide our daily food. The fruit trees in the garden were there for Adam and Eve to feast on. Jesus was hungry, and out of his hunger came the frustration when the fig tree didn't do what He knew it was supposed to do, hence the curse. We could study Jesus' anger and ask ourselves all sorts of questions along those lines, but the main thing for our study in this chapter, is the lesson Jesus gave to His disciples about the authority He had over the tree. We have that same authority if we are Sons of God in the image of Jesus.

Using the fig tree, Jesus goes on to explain that not only do the disciples have authority over the trees, but also over the mountains that have been there for thousands of years. How many mountains have you moved recently? I'm not asking about spiritual ones, I'm talking real ones! An internet search will quickly find quite a few legends of people moving mountains literally, in Egypt and in Assyria as well as other parts of the world. Where are the mountain movers of our day?

But if we don't quite have faith for moving the mountains, maybe we could make a few trees die? Or maybe we could practice on the weeds in the back yard? Jesus gave us the authority and we need to use it, not for fun or for the sake of it, but there will be times in the near future when trees will need to be uprooted and blown away, when mountains will need to melt like wax *(Psalms 97:5 & Micah 1:4),* and we must be aware of how much we are capable of doing in His name; and for His purposes.

Water into Wine

John 2:1-11 On the third day a wedding took place at Cana in Galilee. Jesus' mother was there, and Jesus and His disciples had also been invited to the wedding. When the wine was gone, Jesus' mother said to Him, "They have no more wine." "Dear woman, why do you involve Me?" Jesus replied. "My time has not yet come." His mother said to the servants, "Do whatever He tells you." Nearby stood six stone water jars, the kind used by the Jews for ceremonial washing, each holding from twenty to thirty gallons. Jesus said to the servants, "Fill the jars with water"; so they filled them to the brim.Then He told them, "Now draw some out and take it to the master of the banquet." They did so, and the master of the banquet tasted the water that had been turned into wine. He did not realise where it had come from, though the servants who had drawn the water knew. Then he called the bridegroom aside and said, "Everyone brings out the choice wine first and then the cheaper wine after the guests have had too much to drink; but you have saved the best till now." This, the first of His miraculous signs, Jesus performed at Cana in Galilee. He thus revealed His glory, and His disciples put their faith in Him.

Here we have a very well-known story which has been the subject of hundreds of sermons from a multitude of different perspectives. The point for us today is that Jesus showed the authority He had over the water by turning it into the juice of the grape. In the story of the fig tree the authority was destructive, in this story it is constructive.

Authority and power can be used in either direction, and we must be careful when we use it. That is one of the reasons we must only do what we see the Father doing, and not get out on our own strength.

Not only did Jesus turn the water into wine, but He created the very best wine, one which impressed the catering officer responsible for the wedding feast. When the Lord does something, He does it well and totally, no half measures for Him, and we must follow in those footsteps and not be satisfied with anything but the best. Note that in the last verse in this passage, the purpose of the miracle was to reveal His glory and have people putting their trust in Him. The aim of the Sons of God in our day must be to give God the glory and have people put their trust in Him.

Stilling of the storm

> *Matthew 8:23-27 Then Jesus got into the boat and His disciples followed Him. Without warning, a furious storm came up on the lake, so that the waves swept over the boat. But Jesus was sleeping. The disciples went and woke Him, saying, "Lord, save us! We're going to drown!" He replied, "You of little faith, why are you so afraid?" Then He got up and rebuked the winds and the waves, and it was completely calm. The men were amazed and asked, "What kind of man is this? Even the winds and the waves obey Him!"*

In this episode the Lord showed His authority over the natural elements. He calmed the storm that was frightening the disciples. I have heard, and have prayed myself, many a prayer for storms to be stilled: emotional ones, spiritual ones as well as physical ones. What I think we need to learn from this today is the Lord's rebuke of the disciples because of their fear. As Sons of God learning to do His will in the last days, one of the most important things we have to do is to overcome the fear. It is the direct enemy of faith.

In other gospel versions of this story, the opening tells us that Jesus got into the boat and said "Let's go over to the other side of the lake" *(Luke 8:21)*. Too often we get into a state of fear because we look at the present situation, we forget as did the disciples, that the Lord said "we're going to the other side". Whatever storm comes your way, if God has said you have things to do on the other side of it you will get through it.

If our faith is not yet up to stilling the storm completely, at least we can banish the fear and hang on to the side of the boat knowing that the Lord is in it with us, even if He seems to be asleep! Today's Sons of God will astound those travelling in the boat with them by calming the winds and the waves in the name of Jesus. Creation is waiting and expecting us to do just that.

Before we close this chapter I want to return to Paul's statement that creation is waiting for the End-Times Sons of God to be revealed. This was not Paul's idea. The book of psalms is full of suggestions that creation itself has feelings and emotions *(Psalm 65:12-13, Psalm 98:8, Psalm 148)*, but one Old Testament passage in particular suggests that the earth can get excited about things:-

> Isaiah 55:12-13 *You will go out in joy and be led forth in peace; the mountains and hills will burst into song before you, and all the trees of the field will clap their hands. Instead of the thorn-bush will grow the pine tree, and instead of briers the myrtle will grow. This will be for the LORD's renown, for an everlasting sign, which will not be destroyed."*

Isaiah was prophesying that the curse of Genesis 3 will be broken and replaced with blessings. Don't these words paint a lovely picture? I can imagine the prayers of many a gardener impatient to see it happen! Basically Isaiah is talking about a new lifestyle in a new world; back to Eden!

The verse preceding this poetic description of what life will be like talks about God's word and how it will accomplish its purpose, and the verses following assure us that the new life in the new world is for everyone. This passage is interspersed with recommendations about the right way to live in order to be a part of these things. Although it is long, I am going to copy it here in its entirety because such a beautiful passage of scripture merits meditation, and I urge the reader to go through it slowly and intentionally, expecting the Lord to give further revelation as you do so. It's a good way to finish this chapter.

Isaiah 55:10-56:8 *As the rain and the snow come down from heaven, and do not return to it without watering the earth and making it bud and flourish, so that it yields seed for the sower and bread for the eater, so is My word that goes out from My mouth: It will not return to Me empty, but will accomplish what I desire and achieve the purpose for which I sent it. You will go out in joy and be led forth in peace; the mountains and hills will burst into song before you, and all the trees of the field will clap their hands. Instead of the thorn bush will grow the pine tree, and instead of briers the myrtle will grow. This will be for the LORD's renown, for an everlasting sign, which will not be destroyed." This is what the LORD says: "Maintain justice and do what is right, for my salvation is close at hand and my righteousness will soon be revealed. Blessed is the man who does this, the man who holds it fast, who keeps the Sabbath without desecrating it, and keeps his hand from doing any evil." Let no foreigner who has bound himself to the LORD say, "The LORD will surely exclude me from his people." And let not any eunuch complain, "I am only a dry tree." For this is what the LORD says: "To the eunuchs who keep my Sabbaths, who choose what pleases Me and hold fast to My covenant-- to them I will give within My temple and its walls a memorial and a name better than sons and daughters; I will give them an everlasting name that will not be cut off. And foreigners who bind themselves to the LORD to serve Him, to love the name of the LORD, and to worship Him, all who keep the Sabbath without desecrating it and who hold fast to My covenant--these I will bring to My holy mountain and give them joy in My house of prayer. Their burnt offerings and sacrifices will be accepted on My altar; for My house will be called a house of prayer for all nations." The Sovereign LORD declares - He who gathers the exiles of Israel: "I will gather still others to them besides those already gathered."*

Chapter 14

The Last Generation

Some may ask, "How can you possibly write a chapter on the last generation? What a presumption!" They argue that the Bible tells us that no one knows the times, and ever since gospel times people have been saying that this is the last generation, and expecting the return of the Saviour. I know that is all true, but I also know that the Lord has told me to talk to people under a certain age and prepare them to be the last generation.

In the first chapter you will have read about the events which prompted this whole book, when the Lord told me in the middle of the night that I was to leave aside the message I had prepared and preach on the Sons of God that creation is waiting for. At that same meeting He had me anoint all those under thirty to be the Sons of God for the last generation. Of course they had the choice to come forward or not, this did not affect their salvation, and they could still be used by the Lord. However, if they chose to re-dedicate their lives to the Lord to be totally used by Him as He wanted, and that might even mean martyrdom, they could come forward to be anointed with oil.

How moving it was when the whole youth membership of that church came forward as one. There was not a dry eye in the house! My husband and I laid hands on each one. We consistently did that together, not separately, because we are a mature Christian couple with children and grandchildren who are sold out for Jesus. So many kids of this last generation have not had happy families, have not had the presence of both parents, and have not been brought up in the faith. Somehow, our laying hands on them together was a double blessing of mature parents. Lots of kids today need that.

I have no idea whether the last generation will live to be forty, seventy, eighty, or a hundred and twenty. There are Biblical precedents for all of those. I also don't think we need to be concerned with that. What does it matter how long we wait as long as we are on the right side when the end comes? We can argue forever about the signs of the times and whether we'll be forced to take the sign of the beast or not *(Revelation 13:16-18)*. We can discuss for hours whether there will be a rapture and if so, whether it will be before or after the tribulation. What should be important to us daily, is whether we will be found doing the right thing at the moment the Lord appears.

Luke 18:8 ...when the Son of Man comes, will he find faith on the earth?"

This statement comes after Jesus had told the story of the persistent widow who received justice because she kept nagging the judge. Jesus seems to be asking: at the end of time will there be people like her, people who will just stick at it until they get the answered prayer that they desire? Will there be people who have faith to see their prayers answered? Of course He will find people who say they have faith, who have gone to church most of their lives, who have given generously to the work of the kingdom, but will their faith be real and active believing for the impossible because they truly know the God of the impossible?

To put this in the context of the arguments above: Will there be Christians who are doing what the Lord has called them to do, or will they all be arguing about times and dates? Will we be exercising our faith, or will we be discussing theology? It shouldn't matter to us today **when** Jesus is returning, but if He came back this evening, would you and I be in the right place doing the right thing? That is the question.

Right now God is raising up a generation that will do just that: be in the right place at the right time doing the right thing. They will be found praying for others, making disciples of all nations, healing the sick and casting out demons. A generation of believers who are not afraid of the devil, and who will go all out for God even if it means death. They will understand death not as a thing to be feared, regretted, or mourned over, but as a fast track to Heaven and a great reward.

> Colossians 3:23-24 *Whatever you do, work at it with all your heart, as working for the Lord, not for men, since you know that you will receive an inheritance from the Lord as a reward. It is the Lord Christ you are serving.*

When our youngest son was twelve years old, there was a visiting missionary who came fairly regularly to do meetings in Paris, where we live. One time she came with a very specific message to the young people. She called up all those under twelve and told them that the Lord had said they would be the last generation. It seemed a bit scary at the time, what would it mean for us that our son was a part of the last generation? How could we prepare him for that? But of course life continued and we more or less forgot it, until many years later when the Lord began to speak to me about the same subject. We then began to take it much more seriously. At the time I received the word from God to tell those enthusiastic under thirties that they were to be the last generation, our same son was thirty three years old. God is persistent, and doesn't change His ideas. I don't think He was drawing a line in the sand and saying to those of over thirty that we are too late, that we have missed it, but rather He is saying: *"Those who have ears, let them hear" (Luke 14:35).*

* * *

For those who are interested, I would like to put in a few pointers that confirm to me that we are getting to the end of the world as we know it. Many books have been written and are still being written on this subject, and I do not intend to write another one. However, I must emphasize that I believe what the Lord says when He tells me something, and then confirms it in His word.

> 2 Peter 3:8 *But do not forget this one thing, dear friends: With the Lord a day is like a thousand years, and a thousand years are like a day.*

This is a much quoted verse, but too often it is taken out of context and used to make excuses for ourselves when God hasn't done something we expected Him to do at the time we thought He should. When Peter quotes this verse from Moses' prayer *(Psalm 90)*, it is in the middle of a whole chapter about the last-days. I would love to do a study of that, but this is not the place. However I do encourage you to read 2 Peter chapter 3 slowly and prayerfully, and see what the Lord wants to tell you through it.

> Hosea 6:2 *After two days He will revive us; on the third day He will restore us, that we may live in His presence.*

If we put this verse together with the verse above from second Peter, we could say that after two thousand years the Lord will revive us, and during the third thousand years He will restore us so that we can live in His presence.

I want to suggest to you that we have already lived the first two thousand years since Christ's death on the cross, and at the end of that time the revival began, the Holy Spirit began to dramatically change the church as it was then. Yes I know there were lots of revivals before that time, but give me a moment to develop this thought.

Now here we are at the beginning of the third millennium and all over the world we hear of Christians being "restored" and doing what Jesus told His disciples to do. There is a large movement of people in every part of the globe who are becoming like the first church, and are taking seriously the call to be a Holy People. Why? So that they may live totally in the fullness of His presence.

But what did Jesus Himself say about the last days? Again, this is a subject which merits a long study which is not the purpose of this book, but here is just a glimpse at what He said.

> *Matthew 24:7 Nation will rise against nation, and kingdom against kingdom. There will be famines and earthquakes in various places.*

Has there ever been a time when so many nations or people groups have risen against others? I don't know, I haven't looked into it, but it does seem like Jesus might be talking about our days. Famines? Lots of them. Earthquakes? Far too many.

Matthew 24:11 and many false prophets will appear and deceive many people.

How important it is to know the word of God so that we can test what is being preached. There have always been false prophets around, and Paul often encourages the readers of his epistles to not let anyone deceive them *(Ephesians 5:6; Colossians 2:4; 2 Thessalonians 2:3)*. More than ever in our day and age preachers, pastors, and missionaries are travelling the world, or travelling the virtual world via the internet, and there is a renewed danger that we can be drawn aside from the truth by unsound doctrine. Paul has much to say about that too!

2 Timothy 4:3 For the time will come when men will not put up with sound doctrine. Instead, to suit their own desires, they will gather around them a great number of teachers to say what their itching ears want to hear.

It is very easy via our computers to find what our "itching ears want to hear". It is just as easy to be deceived, and sadly many are, thus fulfilling this prophecy.

2 Peter 3:3 First of all, you must understand that in the last days scoffers will come, scoffing and following their own evil desires.

There have always been scoffers, but now they have a wider audience because of modern technology such as the internet, films, television, and radio.

2 Timothy 3:1 But mark this: There will be terrible times in the last days.

We cannot avoid these terrible times, all we can do is be prepared for them and live each minute of each day with the only One who can save us. Paul goes on to explain to Timothy some of the characteristics of those times.

2 Timothy 3:2-5 People will be lovers of themselves, lovers of money, boastful, proud, abusive, disobedient to their parents, ungrateful, unholy, without love, unforgiving, slanderous, without self-control, brutal, not lovers of the good, treacherous, rash, conceited, lovers of pleasure rather than lovers of God-- having a form of godliness but denying its power.

Does this passage refer to the people featured in our newspapers and on TV news programmes and documentaries? Please note that Paul is talking about people who call themselves believers! People who go to church and have a "form of godliness"! We don't need to analyze these verses, they are self-explanatory, but we do need to note the warning that closes this discourse.

2 Timothy 3:5 Have nothing to do with them.

I always feel that verse should be in capital letters, bold print and underlined.

Once we suspect any of these characteristics of a preacher, then we must turn away and seek the wisdom of the Lord. There are enough people preaching the Truth, we don't need to listen to those who aren't. The only way to test if we are hearing the Truth is to put it along-side the Bible, and to ask the Lord to bring clarity and to protect us from the subtleties of the enemy.

* * *

The last verses of the Old Testament tell us that Elijah must come before Jesus.

> Malachi 4:5-6 *See, I will send you the prophet Elijah before that great and dreadful day of the LORD comes. He will turn the hearts of the fathers to their children, and the hearts of the children to their fathers; or else I will come and strike the land with a curse.*

We now know that this passage referred to John the Baptist who came with the same spirit as Elijah, and did what this verse says he would do. Often Old Testament prophecies have two levels of understanding hidden in them. This one is no exception. It is a two-fold prophecy.

We have no Biblical record of John the Baptist actually turning the hearts of any generation towards another, but we can imagine with the great move of repentance which he started, that family relationships were healed, and we definitely know that he turned the hearts of God's children back to Him. What better healing could there be?

Following this Elijah spirit in the form of John the Baptist, Jesus appeared on the scene, and the New Testament era began.

But can we find a second level of these very last words from the last chapter of the Old Testament? Let's look at what Jesus says about this subject. The disciples knew enough of the Old Testament teaching to expect Elijah to come before the Messiah, they recognised after their amazing experience on the mount of transfiguration that Jesus was the coming Messiah and so they asked Him about this event, trying to get their theological timing right.

> Matthew 17:10-13 *The disciples asked him, "Why then do the teachers of the law say that Elijah must come first?" Jesus replied, "To be sure, Elijah comes and will restore all things. But I tell you, Elijah has already come, and they did not recognise him, but have done to him everything they wished. In the same way the Son of Man is going to suffer at their hands." Then the disciples understood that He was talking to them about John the Baptist.*

In the wonderful way of explaining things that only the Lord has, He tells them about both the present and the future fulfillment of this word. He could just as easily have said "John the Baptist was Elijah!" But rarely did He speak so clearly and simply, instead He used words that made them think, and that make us think too. Before the second coming of the Messiah, when He comes to reign on the earth, we must expect the spirit of Elijah or John the Baptist to come again. That has already happened!

All over the world God has raised up hundreds of prophets to speak in His name as did Elijah and John the Baptist. Any internet search will find people claiming to be prophets of the Lord. Although some of them are false, usurpers that Paul and Jesus warned us about, many are genuine. If you look not too hard, you will find internet sites dedicated to condemning the true prophets, saying that nothing they say can be proved, and that they are lying. I am not going to give you a list of names of the true ones and the false ones, you must decide for yourself. Pray, draw close to the Lord, and listen to His voice for confirmation or rejection of what is being spoken out. If you identify false prophets or people speaking their own words and not those of the Lord, please note again what Paul told Timothy to do about those situations.

2 Timothy 3:5 *Have nothing to do with them.*

Paul did not say to condemn them, he did not tell us to be fault-finders, or to create internet sites and books, thus writing our arguments for the whole world to see. The Lord is the judge, and if they are not on the right side, these people will be condemned by their own words. Beware of putting yourself in the judgement seat, you could be wrong!

Many people who make no claim to being prophets of God in these times are also speaking out His truth. Truth is being preached from pulpits all over the world, in market places, in prisons, in schools, and in homes. God is calling His people back to Him. But look at what Jesus said the last days Elijahs would do.

> Matthew 17:11 *Elijah comes and will restore all things.*

Our generation will restore all things! How much time have we wasted with our theological discussions, our church divisions, and the good works we thought we should be doing? We should be restoring what the enemy has stolen. We should be claiming back from him all that is ours. The word used in Greek for "restore" is also used for "restitution" meaning to put things back as they were originally. That's what Jesus came to do, to remind people of God's plan A. Why did He say He had come?

> John 10:10 *I have come that they may have life, and have it to the full.*

How many Christians do you know who are living life "to the full"? For many of us, things need to change. Satan has stolen the abundant life God intended for us, it's time to go to war and fight the "good fight" against the real enemy.

> John 7:38 *Whoever believes in Me, as the Scripture has said, streams of living water will flow from within him."*

If streams of living water were flowing through all of us to others, would the world not be a better place? Satan has put many blockages on the flow of those living water streams. It is time to put bombs under the dams and flood the land.

We could do a study of what Jesus taught and how we have fared in the great commission, but there is no point in looking back with regret. It is time to look forward, to do what He has called us to do, and that's what this "Elijah Generation" will do. The Last days Sons of God will be those who take seriously the command to restore all things. Then the Son of Man will come in all His glory.

* * *

One of the characteristics of this last generation will be their dedication to Father God. In Jesus' prayer for those who would follow Him, He asks for unity with the Father as He has it.

> John 17:20-21 *I pray also for those who will believe in Me through their message,that all of them may be one, Father, just as You are in Me and I am in You. May they also be in Us so that the world may believe that You have sent Me.*

Unity with the Father and the Son must come first. The last generation will be those who know their God; knowing in an intimate sense, not knowing about Him, but literally knowing Him, How wonderful He is and How marvelous are His works. The Sons of God in the last days will know what God is calling them to do because they spend time with Him in prayer and worship. That's how they know Him. Remember, Adam **knew** Eve and she bore him a son *(Genesis 4:1 & Genesis 4:25 King James*

Version). That's the kind of intimate knowing we are talking about!

Worship is one of the keys for our times, and all over the world worship is increasing. Twenty-four/seven worship centres have already been established in several countries, and many believers are finding the true value of worshiping the Lord for extended periods of time. Our worship is something we offer to God, we bring a sacrifice of praise just as David did in his psalms.

The last book in the Old Testament has much to say about the last days, and in the middle of the scary passage about the day of the Lord and us being scrubbed clean with launderer's soap, we read these encouraging words:

> *Malachi 3:3* *Then the LORD will have men who will bring offerings in righteousness.*

God has always been determined to have those who come into His presence with clean hands and a pure heart. It will happen, and the Real Sons of God in the last days will be those who understand purity according to God's standards. In the book of Ezekiel we read about Zadok the faithful priest.

> *Ezekiel 44:15-16* *But the priests, who are Levites and descendants of Zadok and who faithfully carried out the duties of My sanctuary when the Israelites went astray from Me, are to come near to minister before Me; they are to stand before me to offer sacrifices... They alone are to enter My sanctuary; they alone are*

> *to come near My table to minister before Me and perform My service.*

The Sons of God will be like Zadok; faithfully offering their own lives to His service, not the blood of lambs and goats, but their own lives as living sacrifices because they know, they absolutely know in their heart of hearts, that the ultimate sacrifice was delivered by Jesus and they are ready to pour all their energy into what He asks of them.

I cannot tell you when the Lord will come back, all I can do is tell you what He has told me. That is the purpose of this book. Many prophets across the world are saying that we are in the last days, I know I am not alone. What I am saying is: Don't worry about it, just get on with what He has called you to do. Praise Him for the privilege of being His child, and being alive at such a time as this. Worship Him, spend extended times with Him until you clearly know what He has called you to do, and then "Just do it".

Chapter 15

Just Do It!

Because I have never wanted to consider myself a writer I was not very determined about this book even though I knew the Lord had told me to write it, and I found myself putting the beginning chapters I had written on one side and actually ignoring them. That is when the Lord prompted me to get on with it in quite an unusual way! We were visiting our children in the UK at the time, and one day one of them wore a tee-shirt with the Nike motto "Just do it", I knew I could preach a message on that expression, and said as much to my family. When we left the house, and went shopping in the town, it seemed as though every where I looked, I could see someone wearing the same motto.

I slowly began to get the message that I was to "just do it"! For me at that time, it meant I was to get on and finish this book. Reluctantly, I agreed to pick up my writings again, and I was grumbling to the Lord that I supposed I should find a proof reader for what I had already written, I immediately thought of an American friend who was staying with us at the time and who has written several books, but then I complained to the Lord: "But she will find so many things that are not right, and she'll say that the chapters need to be the same length and that the book needs to be more structured, and... and..." In the middle of my grumbling the Lord stopped me in my tracks by responding, "That's because she is a writer who speaks, and you are a speaker who writes!" I was dumbfounded! But I was also very encouraged. The Lord was not asking me to be a writer, He was simply asking me to write what I speak about. I understood that my friend is a writer, and speaks about what she has written, and I am a speaker who writes about what I have preached or taught! It was a liberating moment for me. Then the Lord repeated those words I had been seeing on clothing everywhere I turned: "Just do it!"

I obediently went back to my writings, but this message was not over yet. How persistent the Lord is, and how patient when we are slow to learn. Not long after this, I awoke one morning with the distinct feeling that I should go and buy myself a tee shirt bearing this same motto, so off I went. Of course the reader will not be surprised to hear that a Nike store had recently opened in the next town to where I live. God does not make things difficult, but rather He does everything He can to coax us into obedience! I bought two!

Just after buying these tee shirts, my husband and I left for a visit to South Africa and it was there that I began to realise the extent of this message, "Just do it"! I had been invited to speak in an African church in Cape Town and as I was getting dressed that morning I had the conviction that this was the day to wear one of my new purchases! Not my idea at all, because my experience to this point had been that African people generally dress up to go to church, they treat a worship service as though they are going to spend the time with the King, which they are, and they dress accordingly. I didn't want my arriving in a tee shirt to cause them to think I was being disrespectful, either to them or to the Lord, but I am learning that "to obey is better than sacrifice" *(1 Samuel 15:22)*, so I wore the tee shirt.

I stood to preach, and after giving a brief introduction explaining who I am, I apologized for not being "dressed up". I told them that the Lord's message for them that day was to "just do it". "Just do what?" you ask. Well of course the message is for all Christians everywhere to just do what Jesus has asked them to do. Many would respond that they haven't heard His voice and are ready to be obedient once He makes clear what He is asking. The message I preached that day is for all of us. It was based on the last things that Jesus told His disciples according to the four gospel writers.

> <u>*Matthew 28:18-20*</u> *Then Jesus came to them and said, "All authority in heaven and on earth has been given to Me. Therefore go and make disciples of all nations, baptising them in the name of the Father and of the Son and of the*

Holy Spirit, and teaching them to obey everything I have commanded you. And surely I am with you always, to the very end of the age."

These are very well-known words that have been used for many sermons, but have we ever actually understood them? Jesus explains first that He has all authority, how vast is that? Ask yourself what it means to have ALL authority. It should make a believer break out in worship to the highest authority that ever was, to the King of kings and Lord of lords? He doesn't just say that He gives that authority to us, He goes one better than that when at the end of these verses He says; I'll be there in everything you do, everywhere you go every minute of every day. Wow! Take a moment to reflect on that.

What a privilege to know that the great "I am" is just that! His name is not "I was," He doesn't live in the past, although He was there. His name is not "I will be", He doesn't live in the future, although He will be there too. The name of God given to Moses at the beginning of his mission to free the Israelites from slavery *(Exodus 3:14)* confirms the words of Jesus above "I am with you always" that means right now in this present moment. If we, Jesus' followers, lived more in the present moment instead of worrying about future things, life would be easier for many of us.

Matthew 28:18 "All authority in heaven and on earth has been given to me."

That is the key to who we are and what we are able to do in His name. In fact, I don't think Jesus was actually telling us to do anything, at least not until we have understood that first part. He was saying "I have the authority, and you should be like Me". As human beings, many of us so like to be busy, to be constantly doing things. We tend to be like Martha and we forget to be like Mary *(Luke 10:40-41).* Undoubtedly a character study of who Jesus was during His earthly life would be helpful. A look at Jesus' personality as portrayed in the gospels would assist us in our search for the Sons of God that creation awaits, and I encourage the reader to do that study with the Holy Spirit as guide.

For the moment, let us look at the instructions Jesus gave to His disciples after explaining to them the authority that He has. They are our instructions too. He said "Go and make disciples of all nations". To understand this instruction today is to look at what Jesus did not say! He did not ask us to invite all our friends to church, He did not tell us to make converts so that we could tell the world how many people came to the Lord in our last meeting. He told us to make disciples, which means so much more than just getting someone to say a prayer of conversion! In fact, no such prayer exists in scripture! Making disciples includes "Teaching them to obey all He has commanded us".

I spent every Sunday afternoon in my childhood in Sunday school, and I learned a lot of the stories about Jesus, about what He said, and what He did. I learned a lot of Bible verses by heart, and I am extremely grateful today for that grounding in the faith. However, I now recognise that the bit about obeying was somehow missing. My teachers, both in Sunday school and in my Christian primary school, taught me all about Jesus, lots of which included His commands, but I think they somehow missed out the "obey" command. Many of our present-day churches, but by no means all, seem to be missing the same thing. We hear a lot about loving our neighbour without any real hands-on explanation of what that means. Jesus' last words according to Mark help us to understand; they are more detailed, more specific and much more challenging.

* * *

> Mark 16:15-18 *He said to them, "Go into all the world and preach the good news to all creation. Whoever believes and is baptised will be saved, but whoever does not believe will be condemned. And these signs will accompany those who believe: In My name they will drive out demons; they will speak in new tongues; they will pick up snakes with their hands; and when they drink deadly poison, it will not hurt them at all; they will place their hands on sick people, and they will get well."*

Jesus does not mince His words here, He gives us a very definite description of a believer. Do you consider yourself a believer? Do these signs accompany you wherever you go? The challenge of the verses is enough, no more needs to be said. This book is describing the Sons of God that creation is waiting for, the ones who finally get it right.

We noted what Jesus did not say in the previous section looking at the verses from the end of Matthew's gospel, let's do the same very briefly for the gospel of Mark. Jesus does not say "those who believe will go to church twice a week". He did not say: "Take the sick to church and let the pastor or the elders pray for them." Nor did He say that those who have trained to be on a healing team must pray for the sick. No! What He said was that those who believe, not just **a few** of those who believe, would do all the things He had done. Isn't it time we started to "just do it"?

Of course, James in his epistle says to call the elders of the church to heal the sick *(James 5:14)*, but he is talking to members of the church community. Jesus is telling us, His followers, those who believe in Him to heal the sick outside the church. That is the best form of evangelism there is.

* * *

As we turn to the third gospel, we find that it doesn't end with any dramatic words of Jesus. We remember that

Luke, the author, also wrote the book of the Acts of the Apostles. (Even the full name of the book is a challenge.) In the first chapter of Luke's second book he gives us the last conversation between Jesus and His followers.

> Acts of the Apostles 1:6-8 *So when they met together, they asked Him, "Lord, are you at this time going to restore the kingdom to Israel?" He said to them: "It is not for you to know the times or dates the Father has set by His own authority. But you will receive power when the Holy Spirit comes on you; and you will be My witnesses in Jerusalem, and in all Judea and Samaria, and to the ends of the earth."*

The disciples there that day, on the top of that mountain, were true believers, they knew who Jesus was, and they knew that the Messiah standing there before them was destined to rule Israel and restore all that had been stolen from God's chosen people. They just didn't understand the timing. In Jesus' reply to their question about times, He is basically saying, "It is not for now. I've done all I am going to do. Now I am waiting for you. Once you have done what I have trained you to do, then I'll come back and reign."

Jesus has been waiting 2000 years for His followers to get it right. Creation has been waiting for the same thing! This generation is the one that is going to "just do it".

* * *

The gospel of John ends in a very different way to the other three gospels. Here John doesn't tell us about the last farewells on the mountain top; instead true to form, John tells us about a much more intimate occasion which was one of the last appearances of Jesus: breakfast on the beach:

> John 21: 15-17 *When they had finished eating, Jesus said to Simon Peter, "Simon son of John, do you truly love Me more than these?" "Yes, Lord," he said, "you know that I love You." Jesus said, "Feed My lambs." Again Jesus said, "Simon son of John, do you truly love Me?" He answered, "Yes, Lord, you know that I love You." Jesus said, "Take care of My sheep." The third time He said to him, "Simon son of John, do you love Me?" Peter was hurt because Jesus asked him the third time, "Do you love me?" He said, "Lord, you know all things; you know that I love You." Jesus said, "Feed my sheep.*

Again, I am sure that if you have spent any number of years in a church community, you have heard many a good sermon on this episode. I want to highlight here what I feel was one of the main points of the conversation.

Whichever way you look at it, the command to feed the sheep and lambs is a call to be a pastor. Jesus was confirming to Peter his pastoral calling. At the same time He was saying; "Don't ever forget that you love me." Basically Jesus was saying to Peter, and is saying to all of us who read these verses, "Do what I have called you to do, but don't forget that the main thing is to love Me."

The first commandment is still the first commandment. How often do we need to be reminded that we are called to love Him with everything we are and everything we have?

> Mark 12:30 *Love the Lord your God with all your heart and with all your soul and with all your mind and with all your strength.'*

"Just do it" means knowing His love, knowing His constant presence in our lives, knowing the authority He has, and doing what He has called us to do, as individuals and as a body. Of course there are many more Bible passages which could be included here, but I will mention just one more which sums up what I have been saying.

> James 1:22 *Do not merely listen to the word, and so deceive yourselves. Do what it says.*

If you are reading this and thinking that you still don't know what He has called you to do, then go back and read this chapter again, start by obeying the last words of Jesus, and He'll lead you on from there. Just do it!

The Sons of God, for whom creation has been waiting so long, will be those who live in constant communion with the Father, who know their calling, who obey in His name, who use His authority, and who are overflowing with His love.

Chapter 16

The In-between Verses

Romans chapter 8 is very rich in many ways: a study of the whole chapter would be enlightening, but here we will look at the two verses which inspired this book with the four verses which separate them.

> <u>Romans 8:13-19</u> *For if you live according to the sinful nature, you will die; but if by the Spirit you put to death the misdeeds of the body, you will live,because* ***those who are led by the Spirit of God are sons of God.*** *For you did not receive a spirit that makes you a slave again to fear, but you received the Spirit of sonship. And by him we cry, "Abba, Father." The Spirit Himself testifies with our spirit that we are God's children. Now if we are children, then we are heirs - heirs of God and co-heirs with Christ, if indeed we share in His sufferings in order that we may also share in His glory. I consider that our present sufferings are not worth comparing with the glory that will be revealed in us.* ***The creation waits in eager expectation for the Sons of God to be revealed.*** *(Capitalization mine)*

In verses fourteen and fifteen there is the confirmation that believers really are children of the living God, and we should indeed live as such *(Verse 13).* Many of us have doubts from time to time, and the enemy is always ready to pull us down. He will tell us we have missed it or we have failed the Lord and are no longer His sons; but if we listen to the Holy Spirit, He will remind us or confirm to us who we truly are in God's eyes.

All of that is fairly clear and very encouraging, then comes the bit nobody likes, the verses few pastors dare to preach about. What does Paul mean when he talks about sharing in Christ's sufferings? There is that little word "if" which is one of the smallest but weightiest words in any sentence. We can become heirs of all that God has for us only **IF** we share in His sufferings! One might ask: Didn't Jesus do it all? Do we have to be crucified too? Isn't the Christian life meant to be love, peace and all good things?

Let us be very clear at this point. Jesus suffered once and for all on the cross for all mankind to have access to God and to know His love. That was enough for our redemption. We do not need to suffer in that same way. Jesus took our sins, and received forgiveness for us *(Isaiah 53:5),* so we don't need to suffer from guilt. Jesus took our sicknesses *(1 Peter 2:24)* so that we don't have to suffer illness. I repeat, He did all that for us, and no similar suffering is necessary on our part.

1 Peter 3:18 For Christ died for sins once for all, the righteous for the unrighteous, to bring you to God.

Jesus' death opened the way to Heaven for you and me. He suffered for us, but still Paul talks about us sharing in His sufferings. Let's look a little closer at that expression. In the Greek, just one word is used: *"sumpascho"*, which means "to experience pain jointly or in the same way" or "to sympathize". We must remember that Jesus shared in our sin, so that we could share in His victory. He did it for you and me, so that we could be with Him in Heaven, so that we could "share in His Glory". Here a second single Greek word is used: "*sundoxazo*" meaning "to exalt to dignity in company", or "to glorify together". Whichever way we look at this, Jesus did not do it for Himself, He did it all for us!

Jesus did it for us so that we don't have to suffer the same things, and we certainly don't have to suffer alienation from God, so there must be a different type of suffering that Paul was thinking about when He wrote his letter to the Romans.

What do you think Jesus might be suffering for us today. I know He is in Heaven seated at the right hand of the Father *(Hebrews 10:12),* and there is no more joyous place to be. No suffering there. But the next Hebrews verse tells us that He is waiting for His enemies to be His footstool. He is waiting for us to do what He has asked!

> <u>Hebrews 10:12-13</u> *When this priest (Jesus) had offered for all time one sacrifice for sins, He sat down at the right hand of God. Since that time He waits for His enemies to be made His footstool.*

Isn't two thousand years of waiting a form of suffering? Years ago when I had three children at home, I could sometimes become very impatient If I had to wait more than a couple of minutes for my children to do what I had asked them to do. In fact we all suffered, they suffered for their lack of obedience, and I with lack of patience and with frustration. The Lord is extremely patient, but that doesn't mean He doesn't suffer from frustration!

One of the other things that has made me suffer as a parent has been when my children have struggled, or suffered in any way. When they have been ill, when they have not understood their school lessons, when they have done something they shouldn't, or have been misused or abused in any way by others. Those feelings are still extremely strong for my offspring, for those I love the most, but in fact if anyone I care about suffers, then to some extent so do I.

God feels the same about His children, about everyone He loves, and that means the whole of mankind. He understands and shares in our sufferings! Do we understand and share in His? How upset do you get when the TV screen shows us starving children, famine ridden countries, war torn regions? Do we pray enough for them, do we pray for the evil dictators in the world from our standpoint of knowing that God's heart is broken because they are in the devil's grip, and not being drawn by His forgiving love.

What about the down-and-outs in your town? Do you turn a blind eye? Do you get annoyed with them? Are you grateful that you are not in their place? Or do you feel for them? Do you sympathize with their pain? Do you feel the love of Father God for each one?

I will never forget one day when a newly divorced father was staying in our house. His wife of 20 years had, without warning, left him for someone else, taking the children with her to another country. He hadn't seen them for three months. The evening before he left us, and after an extremely emotional weekend, he suddenly broke down in tears, threw himself sobbing onto the sofa and cried out: "All I want is the return of my children!" It was a heart breaking scene. Immediately, I had a vision of Father God weeping the same tears, and saying "All I want is the return of my children!"

If we fully understood God's love for all mankind we would be much more obedient to His call on our lives, on every believer's life, to spread the gospel to every person, in every country, in every corner of the world. If we loved as He loves, the world would be a different place. Until we understand that, we are not sharing in God's present day sufferings. We are not living and acting as His heirs *(Verse 17).*

Another way of translating into every day language the understanding of "sharing in His sufferings" is to embrace all that Jesus did for us on the cross. Many books have been written about that subject too, and here is not the place, now is not the moment to enlarge on it too much, but I believe it takes most of us the greater part, if not all of our Christian lives to truly understand the completeness of what happened that dreadful day of the crucifixion.

In order to embrace what Jesus did for us, we need to live a resurrected life. We need to actually live as children of the living God, as His heirs, rejecting everything demonic because it has no claim to us at all. Being an heir of God means inheriting all that He has for us. It means that we get a home in Heaven when this life is over, but I believe it means that we can live in His power today, in this life. Real Sons of God are those who understand the power available through the Holy Spirit, the power that raised Jesus from the dead, and made all of Heaven available for us. We can live in our inheritance today. Remember one of the first things John tells us in his gospel.

> John 1:12-13 *Yet to all who received Him, to those who believed in His name, He gave the right to become children of God; children born not of natural descent,*

nor of human decision or a husband's will, but born of God.

It is clear all the way through the Bible that God wants children of His own. Part of His suffering today is that He still doesn't have too many of us on the earth. We are heirs to all that God has in Heaven; it is up to us to bring it to earth. Much of the church has been praying for two thousand years for God's kingdom to come on earth through the words of the Lord's prayer *(Matthew 6: 9-10),* without really understanding what that means.

* * *

<u>Romans 8:18</u> *I consider that our present sufferings are not worth comparing with the glory that will be revealed in us*

Paul understood the glory to come. He had been privileged to go to the third Heaven, and had seen things there that he could not describe *(2 Corinthians 12:2).*

He absolutely knew what he was talking about, and could remember those things as an encouragement to himself when times got bad. And they did get bad! When he refers, in this verse, to his "present sufferings", he is talking about the sufferings which result from his being a disciple of Jesus. He gives us a formidable list of them in his second letter to the Corinthians.

<u>2 Corinthians 11:24-27</u> *Five times I received from the Jews the forty lashes minus one. Three times I was beaten with rods, once I was stoned, three times I was*

> *shipwrecked, I spent a night and a day in the open sea, I have been constantly on the move. I have been in danger from rivers, in danger from bandits, in danger from my own countrymen, in danger from Gentiles; in danger in the city, in danger in the country, in danger at sea; and in danger from false brothers. I have laboured and toiled and have often gone without sleep; I have known hunger and thirst and have often gone without food; I have been cold and naked.*

When I read those verses, I know that my sufferings have been nothing at all, but I do remember that God is just as moved by the things which bother me, in my life, as He is by people going through the same trials and tribulations as Paul did in countries closed to the gospel. He would rather none of His children suffered, but for the time being, suffering is part of the package of getting the message out to the world.

Many people have been martyred for their faith through the generations since the gospel began to spread across the earth, and sadly many more will die as martyrs before Jesus returns. The Real Sons of God that creation is waiting for are those who will not shy away from suffering, who will not be deterred from their purpose. The purpose is to spread the gospel to every creature. Real Sons of God are those who will consider death as a fast track to glory and not a tragedy. Like Paul, they will work while alive, but know that dying bears no threat.

Philippians 1:21 For to me, to live is Christ and to die is gain.

* * *

Jesus warned us that we would have problems. Why are we surprised, and why are others surprised when they happen? I think too often we have focused on the good things in the Bible, and ignored the little references that we didn't like.

Mark 10:29-30 "I tell you the truth," Jesus replied, "no-one who has left home or brothers or sisters or mother or father or children or fields for Me and the gospel will fail to receive a hundred times as much in this present age (homes, brothers, sisters, mothers, children and fields - and with them, persecutions) and in the age to come, eternal life."

Jesus told us we would have persecutions. He had plenty of them, the disciples suffered from them, and we will too. Sharing in Christ's sufferings is just that: putting up with the same things Jesus and the disciples did, in order for others to hear the gospel. Be prepared for false accusations, rejection, and objections, and don't be surprised or deterred from your purpose because of them.

Luke 21:16-17 You will be betrayed even by parents, brothers, relatives and friends, and they will put some of you to death. All men will hate you because of me.

This is not something that any of us want to think of in our future, but these things are inevitable as we draw near to the end of time. Like Paul we must run the race set before us keeping our eyes on Jesus and we must never forget that the victory is already won. The promised prizes will be given out once we make it through to Heaven.

> Acts 20:24 *However, I consider my life worth nothing to me, if only I may finish the race and complete the task the Lord Jesus has given me - the task of testifying to the gospel of God's grace.*

Paul, many of the Lord's followers and of course the Lord Himself were all called to suffer in some way, and Jesus did warn us more than once.

> John 15:18 *If the world hates you, keep in mind that it hated Me first.*

I am afraid that if we didn't ever suffer, we would never learn to pray. Isn't it when things go wrong in our lives that we turn more to God, and cry "Help!!" Our struggles drive us closer to Him and equip us to help others going through the same difficulties. Our struggles send us to His word for the answers to our situations. And struggles that are overcome, as well as every situation where we win through to victory, all give us an authority in the spiritual realm that we would not otherwise have.

Is there any character in the Bible who didn't suffer in some way? Often the sufferings of Biblical characters turn out be life changing circumstances:

If Ruth's husband had not died, how could she have married Boaz and been in the family line of Jesus?

If Esther had not been orphaned, how could she have been educated by Mordecai and ended up as queen?

If Moses had not fled the palace of Pharaoh and become a shepherd, how would he have learned to live in the wilderness and have seen the burning bush?

If Joseph had not been in prison, he would not have interpreted the dreams for the butler and baker, and consequently been received into the courts of Pharaoh.

If there had not been a tempest on the lake of Galilee, the disciples would never have known that Jesus could calm the storm.

If Paul had not been imprisoned, the jailer would not have been saved.

I know that in every one of these people's lives God could have moved differently, but I am sure the reader understands the point I am making. Suffering helps us to grow into what God wants us to be. It is boot camp training.

The Lord never told us that the Christian life would be easy, but He did promise to be with us through it all. This is part of God's promise throughout the whole Bible. When He sent Moses to address Pharaoh, He told this future leader that there would be many difficulties and frustrations because He would harden Pharaoh's heart, but that the Great I Am would be with him *(Exodus 3)*. What more did Moses need?

When God sent Gideon to fight the Midianites, His answer to the young warrior's fears was "Don't worry, I'll be there!' *(Judges 6)*.

When David went to fight Goliath, he knew without a doubt that God was with him and that He would slay the giant *(1 Samuel 17)*.

Jesus told his confused disciples that it was their turn to do what He had done, and that He would be with them always *(Matthew 28)*. What more did they need? What more do **we** need?

The only way to deal with pain or suffering in any form, whether it is physical, spiritual, or emotional is to stay in communion with the Father. That's what Jesus did. We must learn to praise Him at all times, even in the worst of circumstances, that's what Paul and Silas did while they were in jail *(Acts 16)*. We also need to follow Paul's advice to think on the noble, good things.

> *Philippians 4:8* *Finally, brothers, whatever is true, whatever is noble, whatever is right, whatever is pure, whatever is lovely, whatever is admirable - if anything is excellent or praiseworthy - think about such things.*

If we do that, our sufferings will still be there, but the effect of them in our lives will diminish, and the Sons of God will be revealed. At last creation will be satisfied.

Chapter 17

What Happens Next?

To be honest, the short answer to this question is: "I have no idea!"

The Bible promises in Ephesians chapter three that the Lord can do so much more than we can imagine, and in His name, so can we, His followers.

> Ephesians 3:20 *Now to Him who is able to do immeasurably more than all we ask or imagine, according to His power that is at work within us,*

Please note the last phrase there. His power is working in **us**, that means you and me; the Sons of God at the end of time will be those who understand that power and use it, not for their own purposes but for the purpose of Him who created both the power and us. Not to fulfill their own ideas and plans, but following to the letter the orders of the Commander of the Armies of Heaven.

Can you imagine thousands of people who are carbon copies of Jesus?

Can you imagine people in every town, in every church, in every community doing what Jesus did and being what He was, what He is?

Imagine the healings.

Imagine the crowds being fed.

Imagine people being raised from the dead.

Imagine in every area a multiplication of those things, because the Lord told us to make **disciples** of all nations. So many churches, church groups, and evangelists have made converts, or made believers, but failed to press on until those people become disciples, who in turn make more disciples. We looked at this verse in chapter fifteen, but it is important enough to cite again.

> *Matthew 28:19-20 Therefore go and **make disciples** of all nations, baptising them in the name of the Father and of the Son and of the Holy Spirit, and teaching them to obey everything I have commanded you.*

Jesus had twelve very close disciples, but also many others who followed Him and went on to do what He did. If each Christian I have met had been a real disciple, and had made twelve other real disciples of Jesus, the world would already be a different place.

When we think of what Jesus did, our immediate thoughts turn to the miracles, the healings, the raising of the dead, the water into wine, the multiplication of provision, and rightly so. Many of these things are happening right now across the world, orchestrated by our God who never changes, who is using ordinary people who are willing to be known as Sons of the Living God.

But there is so much more to it than that. What about the not so popular things?

Jesus stood up to the temple authorities as well as those in the nation. He turned over the tables in the temple, and He accused the Pharisees of being snakes as had John the Baptist before Him.

> Matthew 3:7 *But when he (John the Baptist) saw many of the Pharisees and Sadducees coming to where he was baptising, he said to them: "You brood of vipers! Who warned you to flee from the coming wrath?"*
>
> Matthew 12:34 *"You brood of vipers, how can you who are evil say anything good? For out of the overflow of the heart the mouth speaks." (Jesus speaking)*
>
> Matthew 23:33 *"You snakes! You brood of vipers! How will you escape being condemned to hell?" (Jesus speaking)*

These three passages from Matthew's gospel are not the most popular, or the most preached about, but the time is very near when we will have in our church communities, those who will stand up to those in authority. The Sons of God in these last days will be those who tell it as it is, they will be those who declare the truth and nothing but the truth. In all my travels, I have so far only met one person who definitely has that calling from the Lord. He is a very humble man indeed, his calling is not an easy one to carry, but the Lord gives him grace to be obedient to the letter in spite of the rejection he receives from those the Lord sends him to speak to, those who do not welcome him.

So many of us want to be used by God to do miracles, to perform healings, but how many of us are ready to be sent to the leaders in our churches, our towns, our nations to challenge them about the rules they live by, to challenge them about the decisions they are making, about the laws they are bringing into being?

Please note that I am in no way suggesting that you rush out and confront your pastor or your local politicians. We can only do that once we, ourselves have learned to live totally under God's authority. Too much harm has been done to the church, and in the church, because people have gone out in their own strength. We looked at what happened to the prodigal son in reference to going out on his own, doing his own thing and not staying under his father's authority. The end time Sons of God will be those who have learned, as has already been said, to listen to the Lord every second of the day and night, and **when** He tells them to go they will go with confidence, do only what He asks, and will be successful in their mission.

There are many verses in the Old Testament that emphasize this message, but one I like in particular is the following verse.

> <u>Hosea 12:6</u> *But you must return to your God; maintain love and justice, and wait for your God always.*

In the middle of the chapters where God is finding fault with all the tribes of Israel, He still shows His compassion to all, and calls to everyone who is listening to make the decision to follow Him seriously. He is always there waiting for the repentant sinner, calling us to maintain love and justice and wait constantly for Him to move first. That is the call for me and for you and for all His followers in these last days.

Maintaining love and justice is an order from the Lord for all circumstances of our lives. The church as we are accustomed to thinking of it today does not have the best record for loving. Of course there are many exceptions, many believers and even whole communities who have given their all for the poor, for the underprivileged, for the suffering. But I am sad to say that too many churches have not done well at loving their enemies!

> <u>Luke 6:35</u> *But love your enemies, do good to them, and lend to them without expecting to get anything back. Then your reward will be great, and you will be sons of the Most High, because He is kind to the ungrateful and wicked.*

If church communities had done better at loving their enemies, we would not have had so many church splits, and maybe we would have had many more disciples. We must remember that the reward for everything we do is being stored up for us in Heaven. What will your inheritance be? That is what Jesus will bring with Him when He comes to reign on the earth.

So, how do we answer the question title for this chapter: "What happens next?"

Once the Sons of God have begun to be raised up by our Father God, we will see communities changed.

We will see church leaders repenting and becoming what God called them to be.

We will see Christian meetings in homes on every street, and often outside on the street.

We will see local government leaders turning to the Lord and running their town councils on Godly principles.

We will see national leaders spending days in prayer before making even the smallest decision.

We will see rejoicing in the streets.

We will hear praise and worship everywhere.

Is that just a Utopian dream like the dreams of many leaders who have gone before us? No it will happen because God has promised.

Isaiah 2:2-4 *In the last days the mountain of the LORD's temple will be established as chief among the mountains; it will be raised above the hills, and all nations will stream to it. Many peoples will come and say, "Come, let us go up to the mountain of the LORD, to the house of the God of Jacob. He will teach us His ways, so that we may walk in His paths." The law will go out from Zion, the word of the LORD from Jerusalem. He will judge between the nations and will settle disputes for many peoples. They will beat their swords into plough-shares and their spears into pruning hooks. Nation will not take up sword against nation, nor will they train for war any more.*

But as the revivals of the last days begin to take place, evil will increase too. Satan will not give up without a fight, and sadly many will make the wrong decisions at that time, many will end up in Satan's camp.

2 Timothy 3:1 *But mark this: There will be terrible times in the last days.*

2 Peter 3:3 *First of all, you must understand that in the last days scoffers will come, scoffing and following their own evil desires.*

Luke 21:10-19 *Nation will rise against nation, and kingdom against kingdom. There will be great earthquakes, famines and pestilences in various places, and fearful events and great signs from heaven. But before all this, they will lay hands on you and persecute you. They will deliver you to synagogues and prisons, and you will be brought before kings and governors, and*

> *all on account of My name. This will result in your being witnesses to them. But make up your mind not to worry beforehand how you will defend yourselves. For I will give you words and wisdom that none of your adversaries will be able to resist or contradict. You will be betrayed even by parents, brothers, relatives and friends, and they will put some of you to death. All men will hate you because of Me. But not a hair of your head will perish. By standing firm you will gain life.*

Many believers will be martyrs for the cause of Christ. It is so important that we pray for those we know, and for all those we come into contact with, to hear the Word and to respond to Jesus; to stand with Him and not against Him. That is our responsibility as Christians. Many of us spend a lot of time praying for our families and friends, but what about the people who are on the same train as you going to work? What about those in the traffic jam, just as frustrated as you are at the delay? Who will pray for your butcher, your baker, your bank clerk, your garage mechanic, if you don't? It is time to live one hundred percent for Jesus. Let's do it!

But the ultimate answer to the question "what happens next" is that Jesus will return. Hallelujah! He will come back and establish His rule on the earth, and nothing will ever be the same again. Yes, it will be a "great and terrible day". If we read the Old Testament prophecies of Joel and of Zechariah, we can tremble at the prospect of some of the things associated with the last days and the coming judgement, but for those of us on the Lord's side it will be wonderful to see promises fulfilled, to see prayers answered, and to see the Lord's return in glory.

Life will truly be full of those things that are "immeasurably more than all we ask or imagine," *(Ephesians 3:20)* and we will finally see His will done on earth as in Heaven *(Matthew 9:7)*.

> <u>Matthew 25:31-33</u> *When the Son of Man comes in His glory, and all the angels with Him, He will sit on His throne in heavenly glory. All the nations will be gathered before Him, and He will separate the people one from another as a shepherd separates the sheep from the goats.*

The more we pray, the more sheep there will be and the fewer the goats. This is our responsibility. Let's pray and let's be willing to be those chosen Sons that creation is waiting for. Let's go all out for Him, He went all out for us! Let's just do it!

Epilogue

Will The Real Sons Of God (RSGs) Please Stand Up

The word "epilogue" always sounds too final to me, almost as though there has been a death. But this is the word the Lord gave me in the middle of the night one night. I had not been thinking about this book at all, and in fact had once more put it on the proverbial shelf, thinking I didn't have time to spend on it at that moment. However, with only half the book written, the Lord gave me the title and content of this, the last chapter, so I guessed it was time to pick it up again and get it finished.

The word "*Epilogue*" comes from the Greek "*epi*" meaning "*in addition*" and "*logos*" meaning "*speech*" so it actually is just an added extra to what has already been said, and doesn't have anything to do with death, and yet I couldn't get away from the feeling that a death was intended before the epilogue could be added.

In fact, that was what the Lord meant me to understand. There has already been the death of Jesus, the only perfect Son of the only perfect Father, but there needs to be another "death" in each one of us, in me and in you, in order for us to become an RSG (Real Son of God);

one of those for whom creation has been waiting for so long.

The RSGs are those who have died totally to their own wills, and are ready to follow the leading of the Father, all the way to death if necessary. They are those who are willing to "lose their lives for Him".

> *Matthew 10:39 Whoever finds his life will lose it, and whoever loses his life for My sake will find it.*

In the list which follows you will find the summary of much of what has already been said in previous chapters. There is no particular order in the list, it was written just as I remembered things, and it is certainly not a complete list. The Lord will add things to it for you personally as you listen to Him. The list is here for reference and for personal reflection and prayer. It is here to encourage, and to say to those who are called: Will the Real Sons of God (RSGs) please stand up and "Just do it"!

RSGs can say with Jesus "Not my will but yours be done". *(Luke 22:24)*

RSGs have understood what it means to be holy, separated from the ways of the world, having nothing to do with deeds of darkness. *(2 Corinthians 6:17)*

RSGs must be ready to say "Lord I will do whatever you say". *(John 6:38)*

RSGs are a light to the world. *(Matthew 5:14)*

RSGs understand the Old Testament beginnings of their faith, and their personal responsibility to treat others as they would like to be treated. *(Matthew 7:12)*

RSGs know the Spirit that gives them power, power to love and power to be disciplined about their life. *(2 Timothy 1:7)*

RSGs reflect the family characteristics as shown by Jesus in every day life. That means no compromise. *(1 Corinthians 15:58)*

RSGs stand firm against the devil. *(1 Peter 5:8); (Ephesians 6:13)*

RSGs love their enemies, even if they hate what they are doing. *(Luke 6:35)*

RSGs know they may be persecuted, but are not afraid to be obedient. *(2 Timothy 3:12)*

RSGs are faithful to their own personal Heavenly calling. *(Ephesians 4:1)*

RSGs obey the Great Commission. *(Matthew 28:18-20)*

Based on that same passage of scripture, they must remember that they are to make disciples of Jesus, not of themselves.

They must be prepared to baptize believers.

RSGs must not just teach people all that Jesus taught, but they must teach them to **obey** all that Jesus taught, there is a very important difference.

RSGs live in the assurance that Jesus accompanies them in all they do.

RSGs look to Him for everything. *(1 Timothy 6:17)*

RSGs know what nourishes them. *(John 4:34)*

RSGs speak in tongues, cast out demons, and heal the sick. *(Mark 16:17-18)*

RSGs are not afraid. *(John 14:27)*

RSGs are ready to go to the "ends of the earth" if that is what God calls them to do. *(Mark 16:15)*

RSGs must "love others as they love themselves". *(Mark 12:31)*

But first and foremost, RSGs must love the Lord unconditionally. *(Mark 12:30)*

RSGs take Life wherever they go. *(John 10:10)*

RSGs are wise, but gentle, all the time having the trusting mind of a child. *(Matthew 10:16; Matthew 18:3)*

RSGs do not trust in their own logic, but allow the Lord to lead at all times. *(Proverbs 3:5-7)*

RSGs have learned to rejoice at all times, and in all situations. *(Philippians 4:4)*

RSGs must be prepared for division, in order that Truth can reign. *(Matthew 10:34-35)*

RSGs speak only what is truth in the Lord's eyes. *(Romans 9:1)*

Wherever they go, RSGs must serve others. *(Matthew 20:28)*

Knowing that they are seated in Heavenly places, RSGs live by the Spirit, and not by the flesh. *(Ephesians 2:6; Galatians 5:16)*

RSGs carry that living water and let it flow out to others. *(John 7:38)*

RSGs are those who have chosen Life. *(Deuteronomy 30:19-20)*

RSGs know that the word of God gives health to our bodies. *(Proverbs 4:20-27)*

RSGs understand the freedom gained by Jesus. *(John 8:36)*

RSGs understand the authority given to them by the Lord. *(Genesis 41:42)*

RSGs have a spiritual authority beyond their years. *(Luke 2:46-47)*

RSGs understand the need to discipline their own children. *(Proverbs 19:18; Hebrews 12:7-11)*

RSGs know they have the power and authority to still the storms. *(Matthew 8:26)*

RSGs have no fear of death

(Philippians 1:21; Revelation 12:11)

It is a never ending list, a formidable list, but we live in the end times, dangerous times, exciting times, harvest time, and creation has waited patiently for thousands of years, for this moment.

Father, Son and Holy Spirit have waited patiently for 2000 years since the death and resurrection of Jesus for a generation to get it right. Let's not disappoint them now.

We can finally answer the question in the title; "Creations waits for who?" Creation waits for you!

So please.....

Will the Real Sons of God (RSGs) please stand up?

Anne Elmer is the author of ***Transported by the Lion of Judah,*** published for distribution in North America by The Elijah List. (www.elijahlist.com) and for distribution elsewhere by Editions de la Source. (www.editionsdelasource.fr)

Editions de la Source also publishes ***Transported by the Lion of Judah*** in **French**, **German** and **Spanish**. Other languages are in preparation.

Editions de la Source also publishes a series of small **30 day Bible Studies** by the same author in English and in French.

For these and all other associated/similar products please see the two web sites listed above.

Creation waits for who?
ISBN 978-2-917973-28-8
Dépôt Légal (Paris) 2Q2013